You Only Die Once . . .

If the bullet had personal intentions, they could not be for John Wright because there was no John Wright.

A random purpose-without-purpose shot, some young thug minded to pick off any moving target?

If not some aimlessly roving bucket of hatred ready to empty itself, who?

Who had taken near deadly aim at eminent American artist John Swain's head?

Who?

De Lima? *Good Christ.*

Maggie? *Never.*

Both? Heads together, whispers, a recently thought of or long-laid plan. All right, don't run from this unthinkable idea. Sit with it, look at it. Someone tried to kill you.

D1607831

Books by Mary McMullen
from Jove

THE GIFT HORSE
SOMETHING OF THE NIGHT
A GRAVE WITHOUT FLOWERS
UNTIL DEATH DO US PART
THE OTHER SHOE
BETTER OFF DEAD

Watch for

THE BAD NEWS MAN

coming in October!

BETTER OFF DEAD

MARY McMULLEN

JOVE BOOKS, NEW YORK

To Dagmar

All of the characters in this book
are fictitious, and any resemblance
to actual persons, living or dead,
is purely coincidental.

This Jove book contains the complete
text of the original hardcover edition.
It has been completely reset in a typeface
designed for easy reading and was printed
from new film.

BETTER OFF DEAD

A Jove Book / published by arrangement with
Doubleday & Company, Inc.

PRINTING HISTORY
Doubleday & Company edition published 1982
Jove edition / July 1987

All rights reserved.
Copyright © 1982 by Doubleday & Company, Inc.
Cover art by Sally Vitsky.
Photograph by Lee Salsbery.
This book may not be reproduced in whole or in part,
by mimeograph or any other means, without permission.
For information address: Doubleday & Company Inc.
245 Park Avenue, New York New York, 10167.

ISBN: 0-515-09051-4

Jove Books are published by The Berkley Publishing Group,
200 Madison Avenue, New York, New York, 10016.
The name "JOVE" and the "J" logo
are trademarks belonging to Jove Publications, Inc.

PRINTED IN THE UNITED STATES OF AMERICA

10 9 8 7 6 5 4 3 2 1

Part 1

ONE

It was one o'clock in the morning on a Saturday in early March. An Atlantic line storm flung itself against the windows. The two men sat over a bottle of brandy, discussing the proposed death of one of them.

"I don't think fire will do, although in a way appropriate for you," Adrian de Lima said. "Do you have, though, just to spend a moment on it, traceable dental work? Caps, crowns, root canals and so on? I'm afraid I've never made the close acquaintance of your teeth."

John Swain gave him a long hazel-eyed stare. "But that would mean burning someone else up. I don't see it. I don't see it at all."

"An explosion of some sort—but awkward, about the bits and pieces. You're quite right, same drawback as our fire."

The brandy now in use had been preceded by long-ago martinis before dinner, wine with dinner, and scotch and water afterward. But they were both capable drinkers and talked with reasonable if somewhat elaborate clarity.

"There are bridges to be jumped off. A semirecluse like you would hardly make a trip to New York to jump off the Verrazano but there must be a good high bridge somewhere in the state of Maine."

"Aren't you switching directions here? I'm not supposed to be committing suicide."

3

"Oh yes, I'd temporarily lost my drift. But let us weigh that. Mmmmm. Suicide."

De Lima sat in an old but valueless rocker by the hearth. He was a New York gallery owner and art dealer and called himself the poor man's Duveen, but there was nothing noticeably poor about him. A mysterious mixture of nationalities, he was confidently plump and superbly dressed. His olive-skinned face was buddha-bland, his high rounded bulge of forehead as innocent and unlined as a child's, under dark sleek receding hair. He had handled Swain's work for thirteen years.

He poured them both another two inches of brandy and went on in his velvet voice. "The idea has its merits, but I think not. The life force, the steadily mounting, majestic power . . . One might take suicide as a *rejection* by you of your work and that would never do."

The scheme had been tickling away at the back of his brain for years.

Why not, why on earth *not?*

Granted that you found the right ego, the right greed, the right nerve, in the right man at the right time. That was the rub: an almost impossible combination.

In a letter from Swain a month ago, an idle, peevish complaint had been the catalyst, transferring the idea from the back of his brain to the very front and center of it.

". . . and I note that Sotheby Parke Bernet sold a painting of Sisley's for seven hundred and fifty thousand dollars. Of course you know that the poor bastard never sold even one picture in his entire lifetime. I forgot whether it was his butcher or baker or grocer who refused to take a painting in exchange for the very food to put in his mouth. Christ, what a world, if you're dead you're good, if you're alive go screw yourself."

In his answering letter, de Lima pointed out that Swain was well past the stage of bartering his pictures for something to eat. "Consider where you now hang, dear fellow. In the Museum of Modern Art, the Metropolitan, the Louvre, a whole roomful of you in Lily Patchester's villa in Florence, to say nothing of the pairs or singles in private collections in this country and England, Holland, Japan, and, let me think, New Zealand." He didn't add "and all through my efforts on your behalf" but the sentiment breathed clearly upward from the small elegant handwriting.

But for Swain it had been admittedly a long grueling pull. He was now fifty-two, and he had been hard at it since the age of twenty-seven, when he had left his job as art instructor at St. Elizabeth's Academy. He had firmly left, also, his wife and child, and leaped unshackled into work and penury. Trying to find his shape and style and self while he moved from place to place. Supporting himself with the odd job here and there. Portraits of children, lucrative enough at Christmastime. ("What a perfectly charming portrait of Janie. Quite a likeness I do say. My husband will be thrilled. But would you mind shortening her nose a little? And the way you've done the pansy print on her dress—there looks like a spill down the front of it, although I suppose it's meant to be a shadow—could you fix that up?") Large oils of country mansions to be hung over the owners' fireplaces. Quick commercial daubs under another, indecipherable, name, to be sold at undistinguished commercial galleries: clowns and poodles, snow scenes and sunset skylines.

He had settled here in Bride's Bay, Maine, several years before his association with the de Lima Gallery began. He had started his Bride's Bay Summer School of Art and went about the task of teaching with an impatience and boredom just barely concealed.

In fall, winter, and spring, he painted for himself. He paid a modest rent for the lonely shabby house; Bride's Bay was not then and not now fashionable as a summer address. He grew his own vegetables, cooked vast kettles of soup holding a week's dinners, gave up smoking, wore old and battered clothes, and allowed himself only one extravagance: the occasional bottle to be opened and liberally attacked when he finished a picture he liked.

He finally thought he was getting somewhere, at least in the way of pleasing himself.

De Lima thought he was getting somewhere, too, when a mutual friend suggested that on his way to Presque Isle for a summer weekend party he might stop by and take a look at Swain's stuff. He took a good long look and declared himself Swain's man.

Swain knew of him, knew that he was considered a tremendous man for spotting what would be the coming trend, or wave, or fad, or fashion—and therefore increasingly adept at taking matters into his own plump hands and creating the fashion.

A gentleman's agreement was arrived at, that de Lima would have the exclusive handling of Swain's output. Even though, de Lima told himself, artists at the bone are rarely gentlemen. Even though, thought Swain, this glossy man is probably part charlatan, or crook, and devious as hell, but I suppose in his business that's all in the game.

Swain's plaints about Sisley, his "if you're dead you're good," were common enough among artists. But they had lodged themselves in his dealer's busy brain.

Was Swain the right man at the right time?

There was a puckish quality to Swain, a deep dark streak of satirical mischief, which de Lima recognized because he shared, although it was well buried, much the same trait.

Perhaps in Swain it arose from his inner smoldering about the long bitter fight to get where he'd gotten, when the United States patent was, Make it while you're young or you're nobody and nowhere, man.

In any case, the absolutely essential streak was there, and functioning.

In a momentary attempt to put a respectable, even a virtuous, face on the thing, de Lima said, "Think of it like this, in ways you're acting for countless unfortunate Sisleys, paying the world back for them." Hearing himself, he laughed his rich velvety laugh. "But why look for backup motives? Money, Swain, pots and pots of beautiful money, to wallow around in while you're still *alive*."

Swain was only to be a dead man for approximately a year.

Still pondering the manner of this death, de Lima got up from his rocker and walked to the windows. He was a collector of weather and gazed with relish at the sleet, snow, and rain hurled against the panes. And the sea, the near sea, invisible except to the ear, an appalling tumble of sound describing its waves and whiteness and danger.

"Listen!" cried de Lima. "*Listen*."

"To what—that racket out there?"

"Listen to the Almighty God, clearing up our poor little puzzlement for us."

"Explain yourself."

"Your trusty Star out there in the boathouse. A tricky bit of weather in, say, September, a storm coming up suddenly. You ought to be able to gauge the weather after the years you've lived here." He was suddenly and intently businesslike. "Boat capsizes. Skipper drowns. Body never found—after all, you've got the whole of the Atlantic Ocean to lose yourself in. Tragic death at sea of one of the emerging greatest American painters of our time. And, yes"—his eyes rolled and sparkled—"just days before his first major retrospective was to open at the world-famous de Lima Gallery."

His enthusiasm was catching. Swain began to nod. "Yes, yes. I think—yes."

"That would give you six months to paint. Night and day, like a madman. I can see it now, in print: 'Did Swain have some sixth sense of an approaching doom? He had never before in his life painted at this incredible pace.' You are going to make marvelous copy. 'The man of fire and flame fatally quenched in the sea.' "

Glee overtook Swain and he threw back his head and laughed. "But—*what* a scheme!"

A voice called from somewhere above, "What are you two up to?" Maggie Lind came down the stairs from her top-floor apartment, and, yawning, into the living room. Even somewhat tumbled about with sleep, even in an old dark-blue flannel robe of Swain's, she was elegant in her rakish way. She was a tall woman who still kept her dancer's body. Her hair, chignoned at the nape by day, was down around her shoulders, dark hair with a swipe of white over one temple. Her eyes were dark, knowing, and tilted over high cheekbones, her mouth a fluting one prepared to be amused. She was Swain's tenant and, when the mood took them, lover. They were in their own independent fashions a pair, and had been for three years.

She eyed the bottle. "If you were treating yourself to a party I saw no reason not to come down and join you when I woke up just now." She spoke with the natural easy confidence of a woman who knows she is never unwelcome among men. Her voice was husky, with a vague flavor of some unidentified foreign capital city.

It was through de Lima that she had met Swain, at a party on one of his rare visits to New York. She was not only an old friend of his but had worked for a time in his gallery, adding this to a checkered international list of jobs. The early dancing with van Loon's modern dance company, sculptor's model, guide for expensive tours, cooking-school maitresse d'. Then the aunt of one of her two husbands had died in Denmark and left her enough money to live for the time being as she pleased, lazily, consuming moderate-priced lotuses, she said. She was about Swain's age but looked a timeless sort of woman, thanks to her facial bones.

Tinkering with the idea of enrolling in Swain's summer school, she came up to Bride's Bay and signed up for one trial week. She dabbled in a semiskilful way, amusing herself and bringing thunders of criticism from Swain. Then she found something much more entertaining to do. Instead of continuing with classes she moved into the empty apartment on top of Swain's house, and into his life. This was a felicitous arrangement for him, he could use the rent money as well as her company.

"Go get yourself a glass, woman, if you can find a clean one," de Lima said. When he had poured her brandy, he gave her a sharp speculative look. "You weren't standing for a while at the top of the stairs listening with your shell-like —they are, you know—ears to our verbal meanderings down the path of fancy?"

"No, was there anything interesting to eavesdrop on? I just popped out of bed and into this jolly glass." She applied herself to her brandy and added, "You did, though, sound awfully pleased about something, both of you, as I was coming down. Has it anything to do with money? Adrian bearing good news this trip? I'm beginning to run a little short myself."

"We were just amusing ourselves," de Lima said, but his statement went unheard under an overhead smash of thunder. The lights went out. The fire had been poorly tended while the men discussed death and there were only a few rosy ash-covered crumbles.

"Candles, I know where they are." Maggie got up, moving with effortless accuracy in the dark to the bottom drawer of a kitchen cabinet. She came back with three lighted candles.

"Bed, everybody. I won't leave you here with your bottle, you might set the house on fire."

De Lima, a man of the most intense and powerful suspicion in all matters concerning the conduct of his affairs, asked himself, *Had* she heard them?

"Come with me, Adrian, I suppose John forgot to make up your bed. I'll do it while you brush your teeth."

The one guest bedroom on the second floor was a mean little slit of a room, probably once a child's. There was a monastically narrow bed with a dusty, lumpy old mattress on it, a cricket chair with a faded cushion, and under the window a chest of drawers made of cardboard covered with rain-stained rose-patterned wallpaper.

Maggie smiled to herself as she made up the bed, thinking of de Lima's own bedroom in New York. He returned from the bathroom and stood in the doorway watching her.

"I don't mean to look standoffish but there's not room in this cubicle for the two of us."

"Your bed with the peacock-feather headboard," Maggie giggled. "Your Aubusson carpet. Your Louis Sixteenth pier glass. Your marquetry chest of drawers. And now this."

"Yes. Build thee more stately bedrooms, Oh my soul. What an efficient woman you are, by the way."

"Lazybones, though I am, I'm glad to be of help, darling . . ."—she paused to yawn again and the candlelight emphasized the classically hollowed cheeks and the dark, glimmering eyes narrowed against the near flame—"when needed."

Now what did she really mean by that, de Lima wondered as he undressed, put on his silk pajamas, and got into bed. Is she playing some kind of game with me? A games player himself, he tended not to take anything at its simple face value.

He tried to punch some life and lift into the dismally flabby and damp-feeling pillow and failed. He rested his head on it and set himself to think.

Now what did she really . . . ?

He fell asleep.

TWO

Blinding sunlight on his pillow waked de Lima at nine in the morning. He noted that there was, of course, no shade on the ill-fitting window.

Had last night been a dream?

Not at all.

But there were things to be seen to, buttoned up, before he left for New York. He didn't like night driving, especially in treacherous March, and hoped to make an early start.

He looked at himself in the misted mirror and said aloud, "Oh dear." But after he had shaved and showered, the bathroom mirror face was reassuring, the cheeks a fresh pink under the olive. This Maine air, de Lima thought, must be good for me. Even mixed with alcoholic spirits.

He put on a change of clothes from the skin out. The smoky green Shetland tweed suit was new. Too bad there wasn't a full-length mirror to show him the distinguished New York art dealer in country kit. He felt younger than his forty-eight years, and happy. This, he told himself, is all going to be great fun.

He found Swain in the untidy kitchen, drinking a cup of black coffee. "Oh God," Swain said, lifting a wrist to his forehead. "Oh *God*."

"Be quiet and take some aspirin if it's your head you're complaining about."

"I did. It hasn't hit bottom yet. I'm not as well trained as you are in midnight blasts."

De Lima waited on tenterhooks for the "And what a mad idea that was. Of course, in the light of morning all you can say is shove it." But no disclaimer of any kind was uttered by Swain.

Unused to getting his own breakfast, de Lima asked hopefully, "Is Maggie up and about?"

"No, she's a late sleeper, and when she does get up she cooks for herself upstairs, things like creamed kidneys for breakfast, or grilled trout. Oh God."

De Lima opened the refrigerator and peered in. "To borrow your expression, oh God. How long is it since this thing's been cleaned out?"

"I haven't the faintest idea."

"There was mold in the shower cabinet and now this shambles. You might pick up some kind of awful bacteria."

"Spare me," Swain said sourly.

"It wouldn't come across terrribly well—from the public relations and media point of view—if you perished, *really* perished, from having eaten a dish of spoiled sauerkraut or something of that nature."

Again, no backing-out statement. Swain allowed himself an unwilling three-cornered smile. "There's a loaf of bread somewhere in there that I bought yesterday, you'll have to make do with toast. I noticed myself that the bacon's gone green."

Crunching his toast, de Lima said, "When your head clears, there are things we have to talk about. The nuts and bolts of the matter in hand."

"Give me a bit of time until the cylinders start turning over."

"I'll do better than that, I'll give you *and* me a splash of scotch in our coffee."

Swain accepted this beverage with a hand that was shaking slightly. He was a strong, slender man of medium height who in some way projected a feeling of weight, size, and vigor. He had blazing hazel eyes, a fine, large beaked nose, and thick, creamy white hair falling over his forehead and about his ears. He was clean-shaven and had been for several years because he said he was sick of all those hairy bastards. His skin was taut and healthy, rose-brown from sun and wind and weather. His mouth was a triangle, the upper lip wry and questioning, the lower lip full. His chin was long and sharply pointed. He wore a black crew neck jersey shirt and black corduroy trousers. Black clothing was a mannerism of his. ("The world's a melancholy place," he said, "why not wear mourning for it?" But de Lima suspected that another reason was that it set off his spectacular hair.)

"Let's stroll about outside," de Lima suggested when he had emptied his cup. "It might help your head and dear Maggie might choose to get up early this morning and join us. Which wouldn't do."

He put on his handsome coat of covert cloth lined and lapeled in nutria and Swain shrugged into a black pea jacket. The sky was high and blue, the ground snow-powdered, the air cold and gusty. The clapboard house was set on a hill overlooking a cove so secluded as to be almost a secret, its curving arms dark with pines. The sea was still a wild roil, making a dazzling silver and white commotion in the morning sun. At the foot of the hill was a dock with a boathouse at the end painted green and white.

Raising his voice to be heard over the noise of the sea and the overhead lashing of the pine boughs, de Lima asked, "Boat in good shape, I hope?"

"Yes, or good enough to be allowed to smash itself against the rocks."

"What rocks?"

Swain gestured seaward. "That island out there, oh, half a mile or so, Pascoe Island. Don't press me now, it's not all worked out yet, just a rough idea."

"All right. I'm afraid I must begin to probe a bit. Have you made a will?"

"Yes, just this past December. I had flu and when I have flu I'm always convinced I'm going to die. Maggie took care of me. I left everything to her, but of course I would have anyway. Not that she has much expectation of collecting. I'd say if anything I'm fitter than she is."

"Wasn't there long ago a wife and daughter? I seem to remember your mentioning it on another inebriated evening. Would they fight the will in court? When, posthumously, you seem to be getting rather rich?''

''I doubt it very much. Someone, I forget who, told me years back that she'd divorced me, quite rightly, for desertion, and remarried someone with plenty of money.''

''Even so . . . and the daughter?''

''I haven't seen her since she was three so I can't evaluate her character,'' Swain said, his already wind-pinked face going a deeper color.

''What's her name, just in case?''

''Johanna.''

''Last name?''

''I can't remember the stepfather's name, which she'd have taken, and of course she could be married. But they sometimes don't these days, do they.''

''So all we have to go on is Johanna. Did she resemble you as a child?''

''No, or I don't think so.'' And then restlessly, ''I can't remember.''

''Nature does send us these soothing blanks,'' de Lima said. ''What was your wife's first name, how old is she, what does —did—she look like?''

''Chloe. Blond then, very pretty. No memorable feature to guide you, except a small mole under one breast, and that's no help to you I imagine.''

''Well, there couldn't be too many Chloes married to well-off men with daughters named Johanna. What age?''

''Five years younger than I, let's see, forty-seven.''

''Where do they live, Chloe and husband?''

''Somewhere in Connecticut, or did when I was told about it.''

''Mmmm. Well, the only real worry is the daughter, after all, your own flesh and blood.''

''Get off it, will you,'' Swain said harshly.

''Where's the will, where do you keep it?''

''In Maggie's safe-deposit box at the bank. I haven't got one.''

''Does she know the drift?''

"Yes, we laughed about it. She said, What if another woman turns up in your life? and I said, I can always change my will."

"Very forthright pair you are."

"That's what I like about Maggie. Or one of the many things. And now it's your turn to listen to me. Maggie's got to be in on it. I couldn't die for her, if you know what I mean. I couldn't and won't."

The finality in his tone stopped de Lima cold for a moment.

"You're saying hell or high water, wise or unwise, she's got to be in on it?"

"Yes. I trust her absolutely and I think you can too. And besides, once she's an accomplice—and the way I'm thinking this out I'll have to have one—she has a very sound reason for keeping her mouth shut. By the way." He turned his brilliant gaze on de Lima. "Is this a crime we're embarking upon?"

"I shouldn't think it would be so labeled because I don't think there's any precedent to go on," de Lima said blandly. "And I've been doing some working and planning too, about your story when you turn up alive in some as yet unspecified place. Loss of memory. A whack on the head from something as the boat keeled over. I have some distance to go on this script but that's roughly it. The finest medical man in creation couldn't prove you *hadn't* lost your memory."

Swain's face, which had had until now a brooding look to it, brightened at this prospect of returning to the land of the living.

"Crime?" de Lima repeated to himself, and then, "No. Think of it, John, as a well-deserved and long-overdue romp."

THREE

On a morning in May, Johanna Landis walked merrily down Madison Avenue, her pleated skirt swinging with the light wind and the speed of her long-legged limber progress. Nothing out of the way to be merry about, but it was a lovely morning, and she was twenty-six, and by nature inclined to be a blithe girl when given half a chance to enjoy life.

She was on her way back from a preliminary off-camera interview with an aging actress who was about to emerge from the shadows and embark on a role in a musical comedy based on Oscar Wilde's *The Importance of Being Earnest*. Her job was as a researcher with "Dateline Eighties," United Broadcasting Company's ambitious big-budget rival to CBS's "60 Minutes" and "NBC Magazine." It was a good, interesting, well-paid job, taking her here, there, and everywhere, which at this stage of the game she liked. She was well equipped for her work, with a swift intelligence, a succinctly recording eye, and a way with people, open and easy.

She wasn't exactly window-shopping, walking too fast for that, but Madison Avenue offered interesting flashes as she went by, tempting clothes, a sidewalk display of tulips and narcissus, the bindings of alluring books.

She paused for a moment as a determined English-dressed nanny pushing an expensive baby carriage cut diagonally across her path. What on earth was this baby doing on Madison Avenue? It properly belonged on Park. Her eye fell on the window of the gallery to her right. "De Lima Gallery" its chaste roman lettering proclaimed. Only one painting in the window, flanked by thick olive velvet curtains, but it drew her over closer.

A large canvas, about five by seven feet. An abstraction, or was it? What might be flame under smoke, a billowing, a moving, a sense of imminent danger and rather terrifying beauty. She was not particularly interested in art and knew very little about it, but she recognized authority when she saw it.

After spending a minute trying to find the fire underneath, she looked with her natural curiosity at the signature in the corner.

Swain. *Swain?*

Standing there in the warm sunlight, she had what her next-door office neighbor at UBC, Alan Tait, described as a sinking feeling, which hit him almost every Monday morning about ten o'clock after a partying weekend.

The skin going suddenly chill and damp, the stomach falling away, the knees wondering if after all they could support this body.

Could there by *two* painters named Swain? Of course there could, the world was full of the wildest coincidences.

She couldn't remember at what age she had been told about her father. Something disturbing overheard, and afterward a hesitant question on her part. She had been nine or ten, probably. Yes, dear. Your father left us both when you were three. His name was John Swain.

She still had a mental picture of her mother's face, stung pink with reminiscent outrage, tears in the round blue eyes. "Something silly I said about a painting of his, he'd been working at night, he was teaching then at the Academy. I thought it only *kind* to point out that he was much better as an instructor than—Some people who can't actually *do* things can really teach them beautifully. We had what I thought was a heart-to-heart talk about his future. The next morning he was gone. Fortunately we were living then with dear Aunt Ella, because she couldn't get out and about and she liked company in her house. Money wasn't quite a problem for our food and shelter, but still, not one word, never, since that morning. Weren't we both lucky that Daddy came along and after the divorce married me?''

There was something about this disclosure that sealed Johanna's mind for a long, long time to any thought of her own father. She was extremely fond of Stephen Landis, her stepfather, a widower with two young sons who were four and six years older than she. She had what she considered a happy normal childhood, in financially comfortable circumstances.

Yes, this painting was nine chances out of ten by some other Swain. She had once years ago found herself looking up Swain, John, in the New York telephone directory. There were quite a lot of Swains but no John.

She opened the door of the gallery and went into a large hushed solemn room with the walls hung floor to ceiling in folds of the same olive velvet, a thick soft matching rug underfoot. In one corner a white-gowned Arab was standing pondering what looked like a Rubens—a great deal of rosy flesh, a quantity of breasts and buttocks—on a gilt easel. She amused herself with the idea that the gallery proprietor might hire oil sheik-looking men to stand around contemplating millionaires' purchases.

The opening of the door must have made an unheard ping in some farther room. A tall fair man elegantly dressed in gray appeared. There was no hustling may-I-help-you air about him.

"Yes," he said. "Good morning. Delightful out, isn't it? One wishes one didn't have to stay in school and could go out and play on the swings."

Johanna thought that even though her plaid suit was quite nice and her appearance considered pleasing by some, she hardly looked like one in the market for a five-, six-, or seven-figure painting.

In a low voice, such as one would use in church, so as not to disturb the Arab with his Rubens, she said, "Is there someplace where we can talk a bit?"

"Yes, follow me." They went into an identical room, except that here the velvet was taupe-colored. There were no pictures on display, just a single empty gilt easel. The selling arrangement seemed aimed at buyers who were deadly in earnest.

"That painting in the window, signed Swain," Johanna began.

"Yes, are you interested in the picture?" Whereupon she learned that you do not say "painting," you properly say "picture."

"Can you tell me Swain's full name?"

"John. John Swain. I don't know of a middle initial."

How to continue the interrogation? Here's how. "I'm a researcher with 'Dateline Eighties.' Television, you may have seen it. We're putting together a segment on contemporary painting. I'll want as much information as you can give me on this man Swain."

The man frowned. "I couldn't possibly involve the de Lima Gallery in such a project without the permission of Mr. de Lima. He is at the moment away and unavailable."

"But you could answer a question or two?" Johanna gave him her three-cornered smile, which was a charming one. "Of course we'd need Mr. de Lima's signature anyway long before coming around with our cameras."

"Yes, all right. what would you like to know?"

"Swain's age, and where he lives, and what he looks like, and anything else you can think of to tell me that's"—she smiled again—"perfectly discreet."

"I believe he's in his early fifties. He lives in a little town called Bride's Bay, in Maine, on the coast of course. As to what he looks like, I've never seen him. I believe he's somewhat of a recluse. We have handled his work for over a decade. He is as you must know well on his way up, one of our *great* men."

"You haven't a picture of him in a brochure or something?"

"No. We don't," with distaste, "have brochures. The occasional *catalogue*."

That seemed to be it. "Thank you very much, I won't take up any more of your time."

"Let me have your name, please."

For a reason she didn't immediately analyze she gave the name of a friend at UBC. "Margaret Dennison."

"Good, I'll write it down for Mr. de Lima before I forget it. Dennison with two n's?"

"Yes. Good morning."

Out on the sidewalk again, the impulse that had prompted this little deception became clear to her. If de Lima told Swain someone named Johanna Landis had been asking questions about his age and appearance and whereabouts, Swain might run away from Bride's Bay and hide.

If he even knew her last name.

If she would ever even contemplate something so mad as to go to Bride's Bay and try to see who and what he was, this man, her father.

If—even with the correct first name and the correct age and the correct occupation—he was her father at all.

Three days later she was on a bus that would connect with a series of other buses and bring her somewhere reasonably near Bride's Bay. She had thought about renting a car but she didn't trust her own driving that much, all that distance and alone. There was no commuter airline making a decent connection. Besides, buses were restful, you could read to your heart's content.

Getting away hadn't been a problem. She had a few leftover days of her vacation, and she had finished her work on the actress Polly Free and the forthcoming production of *The Importance of Being Earnest*.

No point in rushing at it and arriving rumpled and weary at some ungodly hour. She would break her journey at Portsmouth, which she remembered as a lovely town in the narrow bit of New Hampshire which touched the Atlantic Coast.

She had made no elaborate plans. Thinking about it too much would think her right out of the whole admittedly nutty project.

She was good at popping in on people; her job called for that. She would just pop in on John Swain. If as all too likely he wasn't her man she would try to obtain some material for the invented segment on "Dateline Eighties." If he was her man—

Wait and see and for God's sake don't even think about it

or you'll turn around and run back home.

Her mother, she had found out years ago in a spurt of natural curiosity, had no photograph of him. "I threw everything out that had anything to do with him." Well, then, what had be looked like? Did she, Johanna, look at all like him? "You have his eyes, although not quite such a spotlight effect . . . and perhaps a little of the mouth, but thank heavens you did *not* get his nose. A beak is all right on a man, but I don't see eagle noses on women." Tall or short? "Medium, inclined to be thin. And now if you don't mind let's go on to something else."

She had asked a man in UBC's art department about John Swain. "What's his standing?"

"Well, he's beginning to be spoken of in the same breath or the same paragraph as Pollock, Hofmann, de Kooning, Rothko, Kline, and Stella. Which is pretty good company to keep. Do you mean to say you've never seen his 'Fire and Ice' at the Modern? Tremendous sheet of flame roaring out of what seems to be an iceberg cold enough to look at that your fingertips go numb."

Yesterday, she had gone to the Museum of Modern Art to see "Fire and Ice." A little stunned, she found herself thinking after gazing for a while, My father painted that.

Maybe.

She had a restless night's sleep at the Portsmouth Inn and in the morn before the time for her bus's departure she wandered around looking at the vintage houses with their widow's walks and airy fanlights. It was a sunny day, for which she was grateful. It wouldn't do to creep up on the poor man in the rain.

The bus deposited her in Bangor at a little before one. Famished, she found a pleasant restaurant and treated herself to grilled lamb chops (after all, she was on vacation, wasn't she?) and a half carafe of red wine. Used, on assignments, to being on her own at mealtimes, she ate alone at her table for two with composure. Eating and drinking were good if temporary mind occupiers.

The bus which would take her to Tinkertown, near Bride's Bay, was a rambling, chatty conveyance which stopped every half mile or so to drop or pick up passengers. Some of them knew each other. Down East was her favorite of all American accents and she listened with pleasure to the salty laconic voices.

She had asked the driver to let her know when they were approaching Tinkertown. Now he called over his shoulder, "Here we are, miss, in a minute or two."

She got out a mirror and gave herself a quick check. A combing was needed. She wore a gray jersey pants suit, short cape on top with a white silk shirt under it. I look as all right as anyone running scared can look, she decided. Was it the green of the trees outside the window that gave her skin that odd color?

There was no bus from Tinkertown to Bride's Bay. Calling from New York, she had found that there was a taxi service, which wasn't really in operation until Memorial Day but which promised to provide her with a ride.

The driver was fortunately silent; she would have found it hard right now to keep up her end of a conversation. Their only exchange was about the destination. "I'm afraid I don't know where in Bride's Bay Mr. Swain lives." "I'll ask at the post office," said the driver, and when he did, "If you want to write it down it's Foxcoffin Road, number one-eleven."

It was easy to commit to memory, the address; and very likely she would never need it again. Leaning tensely forward, she saw after a mile or so the mailbox at the edge of the road, 111. "This will be fine, let me out right here at the drive." For some reason she didn't want the taxi to pull intrusively up to the front door. "I don't know how long I'll be, I'll call you when I want to go back to Tinkertown."

Suppose Swain hadn't a phone, suppose there was nobody home, suppose she was refused entrance? They had passed several houses half a mile or so back. She could ask at one of them to use the telephone.

Drive was a polite name for the angling, climbing grass-centered dirt track under pines, with roughly surfacing stone outcrops which must rattle any driver's teeth unless he was at crawl speed. A long hill, a high hill, to climb zigzag.

At the top, she emerged on what might be considered the lawn, deep uncut grass shining with buttercups. The drive went to a tin-roofed garage. The house was tall and white and narrow, facing the sea. As though repeating an Andrew Wyeth painting, from one window a net curtain with a hole in it drifted out the window in the breeze. Moving close to the house, not wanting to be spied and met with a door which had decided to stay firmly closed, she heard from an upper story a woman's voice. A throaty exotic voice with none of the tang of Maine to it.

"Time to get back to work, darling, seeing that you have only what? five or so months on this earth left."

Johanna was by now too ensnarled in nerves to contemplate what this could possibly mean. She had rehearsed the next minute or so, awake and in dreams.

Knock. A bold I'm-here knock. Door opens. Man stands there.

Hi. I was just passing by on my way to Jonesport and I just had to drop in on you.

Who are you?

Johanna Landis. Or rather . . .

The words in rehearsal always tended to stick in her throat: Johanna Swain Landis. It's possible I may be your daughter

But . . . now that you ask, perhaps you can tell me.

Who am I?

FOUR

Bold knock.

She sensed a wary listening silence of perhaps half a minute's length. Then the door was opened.

His voice was impatient. "Yes—have you run out of gas or something? Want the telephone?"

Then he not only saw but apprehended her. Sunlight slanted across one of her cheeks and lit one hazel eye. The breeze stirred her straight hair, cut in a loose bell, very light brown hair with a glint of red in it, the color his hair once had been. But it wasn't the hair, it wasn't the eyes.

It was pure recognition and for a moment he thought his up until now healthy heart was going to do something terrible to him.

"Oh God, I'm sorry," she said. "You look—hadn't you better—?" She put out a hand and took his arm. "Sit down, I mean."

"No, I'm all right." A compressed kind of gasp. "I suppose you . . . Yes, come in."

Yes, I know who you are and I suppose you think you have the right to come into my house, Johanna translated.

"I was just passing by on my way to Jonesport and for some reason I couldn't not—" How awkward that sounded. "I hate droppers-in myself." And then a jabbering about several pub-

23

lic phone booths, a mile apart, both occupied.

She followed him into the small stairwayed hall, which she didn't see, and into the narrow little living room, which she didn't see. Try to find still another reason for this obviously unwelcome visit.

"The other day I saw your 'Fire and Ice' at the Museum of Modern Art and I was staggered."

"It's been there for seven months."

"Yes, well, I'm out of New York a good deal." She didn't explain why. A lot of people were understandably contemptuous of television and he looked to be one of them.

"Sit down." He waved to a rocker. "Are you old enough to . . . ? Yes, of course. Would you like a drink? I haven't Coca-Cola or things like that in the house. Or coffee or tea?"

"A drink, please." All right, say it. "My knees feel a bit funny. But I'm interrupting your work."

"Well." In other words, yes, you are. He didn't move but stood in the center of the room staring at her. His facial color was slowly coming back. She wanted to stare at him too but the air was crackling with something, embarrassment, perhaps, on both their parts. She lowered herself into the rocker in a gangling, groping way. "I promise I won't stay for more than a quick drink, but I did want to see what you . . . what you looked like. The gallery, the de Lima Gallery, didn't have any picture."

She was shocked to hear the trembling in her voice, and the apologizing. He was the one who had left her, not the other way around. And couldn't, it was clear, have cared less whether she lived or died. The whole thing, which had been a story told to a child, was stunningly real now. This man had abandoned her mother and her.

Goodbye and good riddance. Forever. Until today.

"You have," he said, "a rather readable face, Johanna. I'll just go and—" Without finishing the sentence, he left the room.

She sat looking at the braided rag rug on the dust-dulled wooden floor. It appalled her to find how she felt when he spoke her name: a form of second, grownup christening.

He came back with a bottle of scotch, two glasses, ice, and

water. "Fix yours the way you like it." She noticed he took his short, and straight.

(If this was an ordinary meeting after a separation, "Well, how have you been? You look well.")

("So do you. How have *you* been?" How have you been, Johanna, for twenty-three years?)

She took her glass to the window. "Your view is marvelous."

"Yes. The sea is always . . ." He let that drop.

Silence was not to be allowed. You could, if you chose, play the airy young bitch. Mother's fine, by the way, sends her regards. My stepfather's a dear, not at all like you—in appearance I mean. Nice rock, sweet man, really.

Instead, she asked, "Would it be possible for me to see what you're working on now?"

"Sorry, no. I find it puts me off to expose what is grandiosely called work in progress."

"Oh. All right." She turned from the window with a flaming face.

He picked up his glass from the mantelpiece, where he was standing, and it slipped through his fingers and smashed on the hearth. "Goddamn it," he said morosely. "Oh, sorry."

He was so obviously wretched, unhappy, paralyzed at her presence that Johanna took over for both of them. To spare pain on each side, or, more probably on his, agonized boredom.

"The reason I'm going to Jonesport is to see an old friend." Who? It didn't matter, he wouldn't be interested. He's rather—he's enormously attractive, she thought. But was this an indecent, even incestuous reaction? She had no guidelines to go by. "She married a bank. They have a place on a lake but of course swimming in it takes courage even in August."

All she had to do was chat herself to the bottom of her glass. "But how many laps of luxury do you find these days? They both like caviar on toast for breakfast, *he* says it's unparalleled in protein value. Nice to have a reason for that kind of breakfast."

One more gulp ought to do it. "They'll fly me back, they have their own plane, not a Lear jet but a comfortable one."

What a perfect crashing bore she *was* being. Even the most sympathetic listener didn't want to be told at length about people he had never seen and never would see, especially vulgarly rich people.

Why hadn't she at least found something intelligent to talk the silence away with? Because she was in a cold panic, that was why, and her mind wasn't up to standard. She had researched a story three months back on "The Caviar Couple," only they were tanker Greeks, and champion balloonists as well. She had done her work on the island of Lesbos in the Aegean Sea.

"Well, I must be on my way." She put down her glass and picked up her handbag. How did you say this kind of goodbye?

He made an attempt at it. "When there's time I must—yes. Let me have your New York address and telephone number."

She wrote this down, along with "Johanna Landis" on the back of an envelope he picked up from the mantelpiece. She suspected that it would be tossed away after her departure or, more probably, left to gather dust.

"It sounds odd in this context," she said, "but, nice to have met you."

She walked very straight and limber to the door and opened it for herself before he could offer her this courtesy. She gave him a last, deliberately radiant, smile and closed the door behind her.

Get out of here, get out fast, get out of sight of the house before—

After she had reached the shelter of the pines she burst into uncontrollable tears. It felt strange to walk fast while sobbing. The sound of her grief echoed through the trees.

And, oh my God, I forgot to call the taxi. I'll have to walk that half mile to those houses. Oh well.

"Oh well" was Johanna's small but useful safety gauge.

Oh well, it hadn't worked out but she wouldn't have allowed herself any peace until she had made a try at it. Not to have made a try seemed to her sheer cowardice. Question answered, blank filled in. Now dismiss it and go back to what was and would continue to be a pleasantly happy life before his name had dropped back into it.

But the weeping was not yet oh-welled away. It would be easier to deal with if she knew what it was all about. Plain disappointment? Or an awful sense of loss? How could you lose something you'd never really had? Was it wounded ego at the total denial of one's own importance, one's very existence?

If I've caught myself a case of identity loss and have to head for the nearest psychiatrist, she warned herself scoldingly, I will really rue this day.

Still walking very fast, tear-blinded and deep in herself, she was at one of the places where the drive angled sharply when the car turned the angle and hit her.

Grazed her, rather, but she was sent flying and landed with what felt like an almighty crash on a slab of stone outcrop.

A door slammed. "Oh Jesus," a voice said above her. "Oh, Christ." Hands reached down to her.

Johanna uttered a caw of laughter, shock and hysteria momentarily combined. "You could have said that all in one."

"Are you all right? Is anything broken? I don't see any blood—"

He looked her over, sharp curiosity mixed with his own shock, as he helped her gently to her feet. She must have been crying, crying hard, before he hit her. You couldn't get to look that drowned in a few seconds.

"Let go and see if I fall down," she said. "That ought to tell us something or other." She stood testingly still on the outcrop, and put a hand to her hair. "I bumped my head, I think, but—" she looked at her fingers, "no blood."

"I can't tell you how sorry I am." He was a dark compact man who looked to be in his early thirties; then a dark compact blur as haze swept her. He put out a swift arm.

She steadied. "Just reaction. And it was my fault, I wasn't being careful going around that bend, which if I say so myself is well put." She let out a long sigh, found a paper tissue in her handbag, and blew her nose and wiped her eyes.

"Do you think you're able with help to get into the car? I'll take you back up to the house and get you a doctor. Just to be sure."

"No," Johanna said. "No. I'm all right, just a fall, that's all, and nothing on earth short of two broken legs would get me back up to that house. You can, if you will, drive me half a mile to a house where I can telephone for a taxi.''

She was obviously not, at least by accent, a citizen of the state of Maine. And this was early May, not the summer season.

"A taxi to take you where?''

"To a bus station where I can start back for New York.''

"I'll do better than that. I was just coming back here to pick up my bag and say goodbye. I'll drive you to New York. It's the least I can do.''

"Say goodbye to whom?''

"My aunt. My Aunt Maggie.'' For the first time it occurred to him to wonder what she had been doing up there, whom she had been visiting. Swain? Wrong age for Swain, but that was nothing to go by.

His Aunt Maggie made absolutely no sense to Johanna. Perhaps there was another house somewhere near, at the top of the hill? Then she remembered the woman's voice, floating down to her, saying something that didn't make any sense either.

"But do you live in New York? I mean—''

"From one New Yorker to another that's an insulting question. Of course. Where else? Now we need a nice log for you to sit on. I see one over there.'' He took her hand and led her to her seat. "I won't be ten minutes. Do you smoke?''

"I stopped but now I think I will for a bit.''

He gave her a pack of Philip Morris cigarettes and a box of book matches. "Don't move, promise?''

"Promise.''

He thought then, even at the beginning, that she was not only an articulate girl, but succinct.

Reaching the house, he went up the outside stairway to Maggie's apartment. He found her reclining on her cushion-heaped couch, reading a book. There was a cup of hot chocolate beside her, and a little plate of thin bread and butter. He had always marveled at his aunt's ability to make herself comfortable as a cat wherever she was, in this slap-dashedly furnished but gay apartment, or in a near-bare corner with a bony straight chair.

"Hello, darling, a cup of chocolate for you? It has rum in it.''

They had long since passed from aunt-and-nephew to friends.

"No, it's time I headed back. I just found a girl in the drive, in fact I just knocked her over with my car but she says she's all right. She was crying. Who is she?"

"I thought I heard someone downstairs but I didn't want to leave my book. I'll go down and ask, shall I?"

"Please." He had packed his bag before he went into town to buy a farewell thank-you present for Maggie, with whom he had been staying here for three pleasant lazy days. He had settled for a pretty pink luster pitcher to hold the wildflowers she liked gathering; this he found in a dusty little shop which sold bits and pieces and curiosities now called, in more expensive and sophisticated circles, collectables.

Coming back up, she said, "Is that for me? Oh, I love it. She is someone named Johanna Landis. Actually she's his daughter. I don't know if you know he left his wife and child when she was three or thereabouts, and he hadn't seen her, the daughter, since. He was frightfully shaken up, told me to go away and leave him alone."

"The poor sensitive bastard," Sam Hines said mildly. "She didn't look too good either."

"She just fell in on him, out of the sky as it were, no call, no warning, had one drink, and marched out. My poor lamb dropped *his* drink all over the hearth."

"If she'd called he probably would have ducked, and she knew it."

"Of course. Wouldn't you?"

"Well, I'm off." He gave her a hug and a goodbye kiss. "Thanks for my health cure, at least as far as the air goes. I wouldn't call your food and drink exactly spartan. Take care, Maggie dear."

"And you, Sam my sweet."

Johanna wasn't sitting but walking back and forth in front of her log when he rejoined her. "Just testing, everything seems to be working, but my head's starting to ache."

"We'll stop at a drugstore and get you aspirin and water. Suppose you sit in front for a little while and then stretch out in the back and rest." He opened the door of his rented black Mercedes for her and got in on the other side.

"I'm Sam Hines," he said. "I'm Maggie Lind's nephew. You didn't meet her. She lives in Swain's house, in an apartment, and more or less with him—has for three or four years. She told me who you are so that makes us unofficial relatives of a sort."

"I think I've heard of you, unless there's another Sam Hines. Do you write music? Popular songs?"

"Yes. But let's drop me until later—we have a long drive to converse our way through. Tell me what happened up there, or can't you talk about it without crying again?"

What a direct way he has of moving in on you, Johanna, direct herself, thought. But in a nice moving-in way, as though they knew or had known each other and didn't have to bother with the preliminaries.

Not given to rambling, she told him in a few sentences what he had already been told by Maggie. "He was absolutely shattered when I walked in."

Feeling, beside him, her pain, Sam said, "Well, you can be shattered by something frightful, or then again something marvelous, you know."

"Yes. Yes, I suppose so." She put a hand to her tumbled hair. "Thank you."

"How do you want to do this trip, in one Mad Anthony dash or break it somewhere?"

"How would you do it if you didn't have excess baggage?"

"The dash. I like to get things over with."

"So do I. And as you said, I can sleep in the back."

"Good. And I like traveling with baggage, it's more civilized."

He stopped at a gas station with a little general store attached to it and brought her out a bottle of aspirin and a glass of water. "Down the hatch." Starting the car again, "After you tell me what you do for a living, and how much you like my music, you can have your sleep and I'll wake you up for a decent dinner when a likely place shows up."

Johanna suddenly found herself very tired and flattened and not up to being an entertaining companion to her driver. He was a good driver, not using the car as an expression of his personality or a weapon with which to vent hostilities. She had often thought how swiftly and nakedly people exposed themselves behind the wheel.

"First, are you called Johanna? Or Joe?"

"Either way."

"I'll stick to Johanna. Sam and Jo sound like an out-of-date comedy team. Not on television, but on—what's that word?—radio."

She told him in another two sentences what she did for a living and when she came to the word "researcher" she saw before he could erase it the flash, or glaze, of boredom in his eyes. They had stopped for a red light and he had been studying her face, up until that heavy gray word, with great interest.

"And, for a minute, your music. I'm not at all sure of everything you've written but wasn't the last one 'All I Can Say Is Maybe'? And of course, 'Pardon Me, Eve, I'm Adam.' Now I think I'll put myself in the backseat if you don't mind."

"My raincoat's there, pull it over you. Sweet dreams."

It was bliss to be curled under the raincoat, with her handbag for a pillow. While sleep approached, various fragments of Sam Hines drifted through her mind. She had researched him a year ago for "The Warblers: What Are They Writing? What Are We Singing Today?" Hines, not rock, never had been, but contemporary ballads, mood pieces, and three very successful musical themes for films. Not the old-movie image of Tin Pan Alley, the hungry eager man in his straw hat banging away at the piano, hoping against hope that the fat man with the cigar would buy his song. Educated, traveled, rather classy, Johanna gathered from her collected notes. She hadn't been able to interview him personally because he had taken himself off for a holiday without telling anyone where he was going. Raking in ASCAP money, of course; he'd been at it, and good at it, since his early twenties.

He woke her at nine outside Providence, where they went into the Firefly Inn and ate chicken potpie with a glass of white wine apiece. He was tired from the nonstop driving and she was tired, period. Deep-down tired, and nothing much in her head, nothing much to say.

After their coffee, he tipped up her chin with his forefinger

and looked into her eyes. "You're awfully tucked into yourself. For you, that is. What is it? If you've been rejected by
one man—the basic man—you've been rejected by them all. Is
that it, young Johanna?"

"Don't please call me young Johanna as though I was sulk-
ing in a corner because someone kicked my toy blocks down."

"All right, you're as old as anyone, whoever they are. Finish your coffee and let's go."

She stretched out again on the backseat, the motion of the
car, the sound of the engine and the turning tires lulling her.
Sleep hovered again. Funny kind of sleep this is, she thought.
I'm not all that tired anymore. More like a deliberate descent
into unconsciousness, no scalding recent memories to be both-
ered with.

Or was it that you didn't want to talk or respond to anyone,
because for a little while you weren't anyone at all?

She drifted awake on and off. He had turned on the radio,
low, as he had more or less lost his companion. Classical
music, Wagner now, the *Rienzi* overture. Did he steal a run of
notes from the legendary composers here and there? Probably. Everybody did, and why not? The gift was in having the
ear to know what to lift and transpose into something of your
own.

At three in the morning, he stopped in front of her apartment building on Thirty-seventh Street halfway down the hill
between Park and Lexington.

"Don't get out, you're too tired."

"Don't be silly."

In the lobby, he said, "I'll come around in a few days and
see how you are—I don't want to be sued for a fracture or a
concussion discovered tomorrow morning." He gave her a
light quick exhausted kiss. "Go to bed, Johanna. It's high
time you had some sleep."

FIVE

He called two days later. "How are you, Johanna? In the eyes of the law, I mean. No fractures or concussions surfacing?"

"No, I'm perfectly fine, thank you, Sam." And he was glad to hear what he presumed to be the natural lift and lilt of her voice, not that gone away sound.

"Let's see, today's Wednesday. I'd like to verify your condition in person. Shall I pick you up on Friday at seven?"

"I can't Friday." She was not being coy.

She smiled to herself at the very short silence, and looked into his head. Obscure researcher Johanna Landis unable to clear her social calendar for the eminent music man Sam Hines? Perhaps her one and only chance to start something, even if it was only a little something?

"Oh well, too bad—" Then something made him hesitate and change his mind. "Same time, next Tuesday?"

"Yes, I'd like to."

By Tuesday he was cursing himself out when he remembered at six that he was due at Johanna's at seven. He had had a long, partying weekend which left him tired and blank on Monday. His current girl had begun sleeping with another man; Monday, sweetly and lazily drugged, she told him about it. "But I'll save every other day for you, shall I, Sam?" She was beautiful and talented and at a little remove from the

33

everyday world and thought she could get away with it. She couldn't.

Tuesday had been altogether a black day. A song which had been stumbling uncertainly along—not usual with him; as a rule when he was fast he was good—fell on its face and collapsed. He gave the piano keys an ill-tempered crash with his palm and went out to walk hard in the driving rain to clear his head. At the corner of Third Avenue and Fifty-seventh Street, an accelerating bus sluiced him from head to toe in filthy gutter water. Today was the first time he had worn the brand-new Burberry.

Summoning the worst words he knew and having great difficulty in not shouting them aloud, he wondered if this awful black stuff would ever come out. He wondered if Abby, sweet Abby of the loose red hair and the endearing dimples at the end of her spine, was starting to pour herself down her own drain. His telephone had been maddeningly ringing all day; after four unanswered rings his telephone service picked it up. He didn't call the service to find out who was at the other end. Abby, probably. Poor bitch, poor darling.

Heading home, feeling leprous, feeling like one large walking stain, he ran into a man he knew slightly, who easily qualified as one of the worst bores in town. "Jesus, Sam, you've got to come and have a drink with me. Right now. My publishers have *returned my manuscript.* With their saliva all over it. Why are you so dirty, lad? If I don't have a martini right away I will throw myself under a taxi." For forty-five minutes Sam listened numbly to Beddoes' tale of woe, which included the entire plot of his book. The plot kept thickening, and so did Beddoes' tongue. After his four martinis to Sam's two, his listener invented company right now on their way for drinks and dinner. He left Beddoes in blurred but relentless mid-sentence, "and then—well, it's a fantasy, you know, allegory and not pornography, she has an affair with an alligator—"

It was when he thankfully closed the front door of his apartment behind him that he remembered. Oh God, oh no, Johanna Landis. Call her up and say he'd caught the flu? Had a piece of rush work which must be completed? What was it some kind, wise man, some stranger had asked her? "If you've been rejected by one man—the basic man—you've been rejected by them all. Is that it, young Johanna?''

He had no idea what kind of research she did. What would they talk about all evening, Nielsen ratings? Oh Christ, all right, no way out, get it over with. Dinner at Guilia's, just around the corner from her apartment, on Lexington. A movie, so they wouldn't have to talk at all. Tire her out, bring her home. Goodnight and goodbye.

He was still in what his Irish grandmother would have called a taking when, late for so usually prompt a man, he rang her doorbell at seven-twenty. When you indulge a bad mood, a bad temper, instead of hoisting yourself out of it, it gets sourer, stronger, darker, turns in upon itself.

"Good evening, Johanna." He could hardly get the words out.

"Come in, Sam."

He noticed without interest that the apartment was pretty and warm on the rainy night, an L-shaped one-room affair with a row of casement windows which probably looked down on back gardens. A faint scent—toasting cheese? Good God, she wasn't planning to serve him hot canapés? This was the first time he had seen her unmarked by tears, and she looked —yes, very nice, fresh windy sweep to her hair, Swain's memorable hazel eyes, and a presence that registered even through the murk of his mood as sparkling. She wore a graceful dress of flame-colored chiffon with a butterfly float of skirt.

Her sparkle dimmed as she took one searching look at his dark expressive face. It was as though he had brought a thunderstorm in with him, its wind and rain and overhead crashing invading the lamplit room.

"What's wrong?"

"Nothing. Just a vile day." And then, "You must have those even in the research business."

Johanna was good at reading between lines although it didn't take great insight to catch the flick of contempt in his last phrase.

"Look, I won't put you through it. Drinks, then feed this woman, then what? Oh yes, take her to a movie, you don't have to chitchat at a movie." Her tone was easy and good-natured. "Go home and open a bottle or go to bed or whatever you do when your temperament turns on."

He said indignantly, "I haven't got a temperament."

"All right, your just plain temper. I don't think," she added thoughtfully, "that you'd be a great deal of fun tonight."

She had very much looked forward to the evening. She had spent some time, in her shower, wondering what color his eyes were. A very dark gray, it turned out. Underline dark. Having missed lunch, she had made herself a toasted cheese sandwich and eaten it in her slip while she called to memory some more songs of his. Turn on the radio, idiot; one of them might be playing right now. How kind he had been. What utter luck it was that he had come along when she needed someone, anyone, so badly.

He started to unbutton his raincoat. "This is ridiculous."

"No, plain common sense."

Thoroughly out of countenance, and bitten by shame, he struck back. "You're overreacting, Johanna. Just because—" He stopped there but it wasn't soon enough. Color swept her face.

Just because your father didn't want any part of you.

"Do I have to have more than one simple reason for not going out into the rain with a rude angry man? Goodnight, Sam."

He turned and walked to the door, leaving her standing in the center of her flower-garlanded rug. At the door he hesitated, looked back, met her eyes, and then went quickly out.

Dismissed by a woman for the first time in his adult life, he felt rage rising again fresh and hot. He turned it, finally and healthily, against himself.

He went home and followed both of her suggestions. He opened a bottle and after a while ate some cheese and crackers and went to bed.

On Wednesday, the following day, he was to leave at seven-thirty in the evening for Paris, where he had work to do. It was a hectic day, packing, telephoning, dealing with odds and ends to be tidied up. He knew he should call Johanna but didn't want, emotionally speaking, to return to the scene of the crime. His behavior had been monstrous, no other word for it.

Instead, he went to the florist's around the corner, wrote a note, paid for a dozen each of white and yellow tulips, and gave for a late-day delivery what he thought was the correct address.

Summoned by the floral messenger's buzz, the superintendent of the building next door to Johanna's received the long white box. He looked at the name on the envelope taped to it. "But there isn't any—" Too late, the boy had dashed back to his van.

If it was important, the message in the envelope, the superintendent supposed he'd have to go to the trouble of calling the florist back. He opened it and read, "Dear Johanna, I am very sorry. The other 364 days of the year I am quite acceptable as a companion. I'm off to Paris for a job of work, music for a movie called at the moment, *Une Tristesse Blanche*. I'll be there for about a month at the most and will try to take my bad taste out of your mouth when I get back. Sam."

Oh hell, nothing important, just some quarrel being made up. The superintendent, who already had more on his hands today than he knew how to cope with, threw the note away and presented the tulips to his wife.

Johanna was very much surprised that he didn't call her on Wednesday to say he was sorry about last night. That's what she would have done if their situation had been reversed. But then, she didn't write music and he had almost implied that in her field, research, she was not entitled to moods.

Thursday, Friday. He didn't call. She found herself obsessively watching the telephone, at work and at home.

Who didn't? Which?

Had she all the while been expecting her father to break down, reconsider, regret his reception or rather unreception of her, and in guilt about that if nothing else try to get in touch with her?

Or was it only Sam Hines she was waiting for, saying, I'm sorry. Let's try it again, come in by another door?

Neither called. The world "nothing" gave her a chilling look in the face.

Johanna thought for a short time that she was going to burst, blow up, with blanked-out expectations. Under the minute-to-minute tension there was a sort of void, an emptiness, the kind of gray silent unpeopled corridors one would see in a bad dream, stretching on and on.

Anger and—what was it? loss?—frustration and "oh well" alternated. And questions which might go unanswered forever.

Neither of them.

No one. No one who really, right now, seemed to matter. Silence. Silence with the power of a fist in the face.

Was there something terribly wrong about her that up until now she had been unaware? Some projected unknown poison of personality?

After a few very bad weeks, she gave one tremendous heave of the will, part courage and part pure survival, and pulled herself together and back to the here and now.

She buried them both in mental graves. One tombstone, her father's, larger than the other and more distant one. Get on with it. With what?

Early in June, her chief, Jack Feroni, said, "I have a juicy thing for you, Jo."

"What's that?" Do sound interested, eager.

"Ireland. A rich American bought a whole town piece by piece in secret, and has now set himself up there as a sort of king. Town in rebellion, fists and fires and pubs boiling over with speeches. Enjoy yourself."

When he got back from Paris in the middle of June, Sam Hines made several dozen re-entry telephone calls. Then there was a tickle at the back of his mind. Who—? Oh, Johanna. Johanna Landis. He tried her home phone number in the evening and got no answer. He had no idea where she worked; either he'd forgotten or never let her get far enough to tell him.

He remembered, at dinner on the way down from Bride's Bay, asking her about her stepfather. Did she like him? Yes, she did. He thought she had talked a little about him, and hadn't she said he had his own law firm?

He found Landis and Landis, 12 Chambers Street, in the telephone directory. "Which Mr. Landis?" asked the switchboard operator.

"Any Mr. Landis will do."

A young man's voice, couldn't be her stepfather. "Walter Landis, what can I do for you?"

Sam identified himself. "I'm trying to reach Johanna, I assume she's your Landis one way or the other. I can't recall where she works."

"United Broadcasting on East Fifty-sixth Street. I'll give you the number, wait a second. I'm her brother. She may be out of the country, she often is."

Johanna Landis, he was informed by UBC, was in Ireland on assignment. Any idea when she would be back? No, sorry. Is it important? Would you like to leave your name and phone number in that case? No, thank you.

Well, he had tried. But she was still there, somewhere, in his head. Unfinished business of some sort. And perhaps important after all.

SIX

"I can't have people swarming all over this house," Swain complained to Maggie. "Can't you head him off?"

"First, Matt hardly constitutes a swarm, and second, he's coming to see me, not you." Maggie got up to stir her shrimps, browning in butter, shallots, and lemon rind." And no, I can't head him off or rather won't. Poor darling, he's probably planning to borrow money from me. He still hasn't found a job."

Matthew Cummings was the second of Maggie's two husbands. They had been divorced for six years but had not broken off contact. Maggie was too good-natured to turn her back firmly on him, and he was, or thought he was, still in love with her. Or more probably thinks he needs me, Maggie summed it up to herself. And of course he does. But if you gave away bits and pieces of yourself to everybody in the world who needed you there wouldn't be anything left of your own. And he had been an impossible man, with his tantrums and his drinking, to live with; although she had managed five years of it.

The job he had lost three months ago had been with a public relations firm. He was a capable man at whatever he did and his occasional drinking bouts, in a field often fueled on alcohol, were not a major contributory factor to his firing. Money was getting tighter everywhere and when you had to

40

cut thirty thousand dollars out of the salary budget you did not fire a man in his thirties when you could hack off a man of forty-eight, over the hill in this business which depended so much on facades.

"He's probably," Maggie went on, "borrowed the last penny he can get from everyone he knows. I'm usually the last stop. Which you must admit is thoughtful of him."

Swain was no longer listening to her. He was thinking, as he often did at unexpected moments, of his daughter, Johanna. He had been tempted a dozen times to pick up the telephone and call her. Talk to her. She had looked and sounded like an awfully, yes, nice girl. It was strange, jolting, to see your own eyes looking back at you, and surely something of yourself moving, speaking—existing.

But this wasn't the time to make any kind of connection with her, not when, in a few months, she would be presented with his death. Perhaps when the death was all over and done with—

"Come back, Johnny, from wherever you've gone away to. Your shrimps are ready."

It was rarely now that he allowed himself a sit-down drink and dinner with her. He was caught up in a passion of work, fighting the clock. Almost, he told himself, as if you are really going to die, you bloody fool. Die in September. But the urgency, the deadline—apt word to keep in mind—was enormously stimulating and productive. He thought he had never worked so well and fast and adventurously in his life. Last night he had painted until three in the morning, totally unaware of the time, and had gotten up at eight fresh and eager.

He refused a brandy with his coffee. "I've got to get back to it."

"Don't work too late. Or, what am I saying, *do* work too late. Not long left, now," Maggie said.

Matt wasn't due until around one, and he was usually good about sticking to times. Maggie applied herself to her usual delightful morning. Shortly after she moved in, Swain accused her of being an outright hedonist. "A lot more people would be, if only they knew how," Maggie said. "It takes a certain knack to simply enjoy yourself.''

She rose at nine, had two cups of aromatic black coffee made from an Italian after-dinner grind, and in her leotard did her cat-stretching ballet exercises to music. A grilled lamb kidney for breakfast, lovely, and enough protein in it to take you right through the day; if, that is, you hadn't her appetite. She ate an orange and an apple while she read a leftover section of last Sunday's New York *Times*. Then down to the crescent of the beach, in the morning sun, to walk in the sand, so good for one's feet, the exercise and the cosmetic pumice rubbing of the sand on the skin.

She inhaled the bright crystal salt air with great pleasure. Walk a minute ankle-deep in the calm sea, for the icy thrill of it. Then, sensuous contrast, strip to the skin and lie down on the dock for a sunbath. The cove was completely private and there was no one but Swain to look down on her from on top. It was too early in the season for near-in boat traffic and she wouldn't in any case have cared if she was spotted by somebody under sail. She was still lithe. Small-breasted bodies, she told herself as she affectionately stroked her rib cage, warm in the sun, aged better than the more voluptuous variety. A half hour would do it; mustn't dry out the skin oils. And the breeze, picking up, was a little cool.

At eleven she bicycled into Bride's Bay with the idea of picking up something for lunch if Matt arrived hungry. She bought two fresh-caught Spanish mackerel, and bicycled on to a house where a woman named Mrs. Clist had fresh-baked bread and fresh-laid eggs for sale. The fish, she thought, just broiled, too good for anything but plain cooking; and perhaps a currant jelly omelette and a small tart green salad. Her mouth was watering. Even if he wasn't hungry, her own little feast lay temptingly in the near future.

She never went near Swain in the morning. He painted in the barn behind the house, into the north wall of which he had had an immense window installed. In midsummer he turned on his dusty electric fan and in winter inadequately warmed the great space with two kerosene heaters. The barn doors were indeed a blessing when there was a finished painting to be removed; the canvas he was working on now measured ten by fourteen feet. But none, in the past four months, had been removed. The immense standing stacks against two walls were beginning to make Swain feel claustrophobic.

Matt arrived at a quarter to one, in a taxi from Tinkertown. "This is a hell of a place to get to," he said, winded after climbing the outside stairway.

"You say that every time you come here but it still doesn't keep you away. Hello, darling."

Matt Cummings was a little shorter than she, with a close-knit toughly muscled build. He was balding, over his fierce black brows and protuberant and often irascible blue eyes. Bitterness had begun to shape his mouth, which when he was younger had a certain sweetness to it. Not by any means a handsome man, with his large nose, chunky and cleft at the end. When she had married him, Maggie had been asked by her friends, But what did she see in him? Maggie said she supposed she found him sexy.

He had been, in his career of sudden violent job changes (a shouting quarrel with his employer, or a feeling that someone had been unfairly jumped over his head, or other powerful personal explosions) a reporter for the *Times*, an advertising copywriter, an editor on three different trade publications, pursuits where he was always at the edge, never at the throbbing center. When in time he got close to the center something inevitably blew up.

"Are you in drinking condition, Matt?" Sometimes he didn't dare touch it, sometimes it was more or less under control, and sometimes he just didn't give a damn.

"Yes, no sweat. That son of a bitch gets me all the way up to a nowhere Maine town for a chat and then tells me he couldn't possibly afford a man of my stature. And I always thought I was a short goddamn littlebritches." The man he referred to was a friend from his *Times* days who had bought a small-town newspaper; Matt had hoped to squeeze a job from him. "Christ, I could run the whole operation with my eyes closed, he could go home and play Ping-Pong. Thanks, Maggie, cheers."

"Anything else good in sight?" Maggie took her drink to the stove and put a generous cube of butter into her black iron frying pan.

He was sitting at the kitchen table, watching her with several

kinds of hunger. She wore cream-colored drill pants, beautifully cut, and a scarlet turtleneck jersey. Her high-arched feet
were bare. Sunlight hit and glowed on the white swipe in her
dark hair.

"Yes, and you put it just right. You. Why not another
whack at it, Maggie?" He gave her his grin, which had once
been mirthful and now was a little twisted. "With your money
and my brains and aging charms it would be the perfect solution as far as I'm concerned. I could work on my play and—"

Matt's play. Maggie felt an inward half smile and half
sadness. He had been working on it, or more often talking
about working on it, for a decade. He had read her, late on
drinking nights during their marriage, bits and portions of
scenes, read them loudly and excitedly, his face very red.

"I see this as an absolute killer of a second-act curtain."

"But you haven't even finished the first act."

"Jesus, Maggie, what do you think I'm doing, some trudge-
along job like painting a wall or building bookshelves? You
don't understand how the creative mind leaps here and there
at will. And besides, I've completely scrapped the first act, so
why let that pin me down?"

Now, she said, "No, Matt. Honestly and absolutely no.
You seem to forget, along with everything else, a man named
Swain."

"*You* were able to forget a man named Cummings," he
said. "And a lot of other men, a husband and whatnot, along
the way. You're in good practice, Maggie my love."

"I'm sorry, Matt." A quenching, soft, and final answer.

After lunch she said, "You look awfully tired, were you up
late?"

"Yes, three or so, I couldn't sleep."

"I'm going to see you off to a nap—that long trip ahead of
you." She persuaded him onto the couch, protesting and
reaching for her. She covered him with a light blanket, and got
hastily out of the house.

She had a nice long wander in the woods, in the cathedral
hushing and towering of the pines, breathing their incense.
Poor Matt. He would want to stay all night, of course. He
always had to be firmly ordered out and home. Swain was

casual enough in his ways with her but he wouldn't put up with that.

When she got back he was up, drinking the last of the after-lunch coffee. "Surly fellow, Swain, isn't he. Not even the courtesy to show his face to a visitor."

"My dear contentious Matt. You don't want to see him and now you're railing because you haven't."

"It's too much to suppose that he's jealous and furious that I'm here with you. He'd know you've reduced me to a eunuch."

"Do stop ranting. He's working very hard, against time." She caught herself.

"Against what time? Some kind of smartass New York show?"

"There's talk of one."

"Well, when you see him, give him my worst."

He hesitated and then, all curled over inside—ask the most and expect the least, if anything at all— "To be going on with, could you part with a thousand?"

"I can let you have"— Maggie got her checkbook from the desk—"five hundred. Which is frankly straining things a bit. Where by the way are you staying?"

"Right now, with Joe Rainey. But he's an opinionated bastard and I don't know how much longer I can stand him."

Maggie grinned. "Opinionated meaning his opinions aren't the same as yours." She wrote the check and handed it to him. "It might be a good idea to stay with your newspaper friend tonight and then have the day to get comfortably back to New York."

"He did ask me to stay for a couple of days. To pick my brains, probably." He wanted to further abuse Arthur Connelly, but a deep weariness stilled his tongue. He went to the telephone and called his taxi. "You don't want me here, you have more festive things to occupy yourself with."

"Don't be silly. There may be some kind of awfully good news waiting in the wings for you. I suppose you're listed with all the good placement people?"

"Yes, have been for months."

Fortunately the taxi was prompt. At her door, he turned.

There were tears in his prominent blue eyes. "Bear me in mind, Maggie, remember that I exist—or I hope I still do—in case you and Swain ever . . ." The tears made him blink.

He started down the stairs and his final words, sounding as if they were being slowly torn from him, were, "I am, you know, Maggie in . . . every . . . way . . . desperate."

SEVEN

It was at the dentist's that Alice Smith made her interesting discovery.

She was sitting in the waiting room along with three other people, two of them men, one of them not bad-looking. Resigned to being stuck in her chair for at least twenty minutes, she never got in to Dr. Marble sooner than that, she inspected the magazines on the table beside her. *Good Housekeeping.* *Boy's Life.* An old *Newsweek*, May 10. A much-thumbed comic book, *The Green Goon. Art Today*.

It would be nice to be observed by the not bad-looking man across from her picking up *Art Today* and browsing through it. You'd certainly be taken as a person of culture, not one of the usual nobodies sitting around at the dentist's. Or, equally pleasant, he might think, You wouldn't expect a pretty girl like that to be interested in art.

It was hard going, though. She fought a yawn and stared at a photograph of a piece of sculpture in front of the Trant Building in New York. It looks, she thought, like a person's intestines, although she had only the vaguest idea of the appearance of intestines. But anyway, squirmy. She turned the page. "New Acquisitions at London's National Gallery." A name jumped up off the page at her. John Swain. The caption under the picture of his painting read, "John Swain goes from power to power. This is his 'Number Fifty.' " Funny kind of picture, all smoky grays and powdery blues, a sift of sulphur yellow in one corner, and near the bottom, to the left, a little searing glimpse of fiery red that seemed to come and go as you looked at it.

Could it be the same John Swain? Could it be her own *father*, here in this magazine?

Her Aunt Daisy had told her about it, after one can of beer too many, a few years ago. "It's not everybody that can call themselves a love child." It had come as a sort of shock at first. I mean, thought Alice, who likes to find out they're illegitimate? But then it became to seem rather romantic, exciting, and put her in a special category far and above her sister, Jen, and brother, Billy. No wonder she felt different from those two. Looked different too. Finer, she had always told herself. Jen with that sallow oily skin and Billy with his face all pitted from acne.

The man, John Swain, was an artist, Daisy said, and to clarify this, "He painted paintings." He had, well, lived with her mother for a month, that time her father was off on a construction job in Delaware. "You were a premature baby," said Daisy with a wink. "But that's common enough. Naturally Swain moved out before your let's say father came home."

"Didn't she ever try to get in touch with him? With Swain?"

"Would *you*, under the circumstances? She probably knew all along what she was doing. She looked up to him, she'd never had a man like that around. Clever, and funny. Class, you know. Good-looking in his way. Penniless, but I guess most artists are."

"So you met him."

"We never had any secrets from each other and I think she wanted to show him off. He was like, you know, a little island in her life. She could always go back to it in her head. I don't think she was all that crazy about Charlie, ever. But in our day the great thing to do was get married. I must say you kids have it made."

No wonder, Alice thought with immense gratification, that she had always been her mother's favorite. Her mother had been dead for three years; shame they hadn't been able to talk

together about this fascinating man. I suppose, Alice decided,
I'm more or less an aristocrat. *Well.*

It hadn't occurred to her at the time to do anything about
this disclosure. It was just a nice thing to know. He could be
anywhere in the country or for that matter anywhere in the
world. Or he could be dead.

But now she could hardly wait to get home and tell Stanley
about the picture of the painting in the magazine. She was in
the process of having a discolored front tooth capped and she
thought there would be no end to the whistling of the instru-
ment honing the tooth down.

Why, he must be a famous man. The National Gallery,
London. Was he English, then? Daisy hadn't said.

"You are my favorite patient," Dr. Marble told her, when
he stopped honing for today. "Such a good girl in the chair.
So brave."

She looked up at him with large clear blue eyes. "Aren't you
sweet, Dr. Marble. But then, it's not me, it's just that you're
so gentle."

She would never know, but she was a nearly perfect repro-
duction of John Swain's maternal Aunt Carlotta. Up to and
including the delicate good-girlishness underlaid with steel.

It was four-thirty when she left the dentist's. She had been
excused for the afternoon from her work at Berlin's Department Store in Trenton, where she was secretary to the president, Mr. Berlin. Joe, she called him when there was no one
else around. They had had one motel weekend together, when
Stanley had to go to a convention of disc jockeys in Buffalo.
But she wasn't in a hurry to repeat it. I am not, Mr. Berlin, all
that available.

She and Stanley Parker had been sharing for six months a
garden apartment in Yardville, only a few miles' drive from
Trenton. Stanley worked there too, at Station WKKI, which
translated the call letters into the word "wacky" in its advertising and promotion. He was on one of his crazy shifts this
week, four in the morning until twelve noon, and he had just
gotten up and was drinking his coffee.

He was twenty-nine to her twenty-five, a tall man, bulky
and heavy-thighed in his jeans. He had the near-inevitable
long sweeping mustache and beard of his tribe, and affected

the currently popular western look. Fancy leather boots, heeled, a chamois shirt, a Stetson waiting on the hall table to be put on. A certain hardness of the dark eyes contrasted with the plump pink of his lips. Alice found him in every way extremely attractive.

"Cup of coffee for you?"

"No, yes—wait till I tell you." She went into the bedroom to change out of her seersucker suit into a long flowered dress tied about the waist with ribbon.

She hadn't until now told Stanley about her real father. Some people might feel it was, well, funny, to be illegitimate. He interrupted this opening with a delighted grin and a "Well, you little bastard, you." "Stop it, Stanley. And this is just for your ears, no one else's." She went eagerly on with her tale.

Stanley was at first inclined to dismiss it. "Have you any real proof this guy is your father?"

"No, but Aunt Daisy says so."

"Look, if she was shacked up with him while your old man was away, she might have had other bedmates too. I mean, if every girl I ever—let's not go into that, but I'd say, hell, that was the man last night, that wasn't me."

Alice didn't like the turn the conversation was taking. Crude.

"What kind of money do you think he'd get for that painting?" Stanley, wolfing toasted English muffins, showed a flicker of interest.

"I don't know, but maybe a lot. And maybe he's sold, oh, dozens and dozens."

"Maybe he's rich?" Stanley asked softly.

"Could be."

"And you think he'd like to share some of it with you?" Stanley allowed himself a shout of laughter. "That is, if you can find him?"

"I don't see why not," said Alice in her clear, quiet, determined way.

"Well, work on it," he advised tolerantly. "And I'll mull it over, maybe come up with some way of helping you out. Who knows? I have good reason to believe that when you really want something there's no stopping you."

• • •

Adrian de Lima walked to one of the two doors in his large office, opened it, and put his head into the smaller office. He could have summoned by buzzer his secretary, Lucy Delft, but he considered this one of the many discourteous habits of the twentieth century.

"A project for you, Lucy. And right at sherry time too, isn't that nice?"

It was eleven o'clock on a hot gray July morning; hot outside, that is; cool as May inside. Lucy, a distinguished, bony, silvery woman in her forties, got up from her desk and preceded him into his office, which looked like a living room in a country house. No desk at all; when de Lima wished to attend to papers, he did so at an antique music stand. He poured two glasses of sherry from a Waterford decanter and produced a box of Fauchon lime biscuits.

"Now then. A man I know wants to leave his present place of residence and live for a year in total obscurity."

Bizarre tasks for de Lima were nothing new to Lucy. "Total obscurity," she repeated thoughtfully. "You're not thinking of Europe, a monastery?"

"No, no. I think I can best define it, the place he wants, as a quiet, off-the-path, nowhere place. And modest. He doesn't want to put out a lot of money."

By coincidence, Lucy had spent last weekend with her cousin Helena at Helena's little box of a screen-porched house at Seashell Park, New Jersey.

"What time period are we talking about?"

"Say, sometime in September to start his year."

"The most nowhere place I can think of is one of those littery little seaside resort towns on the Jersey coast, particularly nowhere after Labor Day."

"Ah." De Lima sipped his sherry and thought about this. "Not too far from Maggie," Swain had said. "I'd go mad if I couldn't rely on her occasional visit." "But there are planes, dear fellow." "No. I want her to be able to come and go on impulse, whenever she feels like it, not turn herself into a travel bureau."

"Had you any specific place in mind, in your nowhere?" he asked Lucy.

"Yes. My cousin Helena has a house, *very* modest. She tries to rent it every year after Labor Day but of course there are seldom any takers. The town is called Seashell Park. It is not"—her nostrils flared in recollection—"in any remotest way to be taken as grand. Little places cheek by jowl, sandy yards, clotheslines, hardly any trees. The sea a few blocks away, a boardwalk with far up at one end an amusement park reeking of mustard and popcorn oil."

De Lima shuddered. "I see it all. Practically deserted after the season, I take it?"

"Yes. She spent one winter there three years ago—she'd been ill and thought the sea air would help—and I went down to see her. The store was open, the grocery and liquor store, but not much else. I suppose about a third of the houses were occupied, mostly by elderly people, probably retired."

"Sea air. Health. Walks on the beach needed. Mmmmm. I like it. But what happens when Memorial Day rolls around, where does our man go then?"

"There's plenty of time to deal with that. Although Helena has a terrible old white elephant of a house in a neighborhood in Philadelphia which has turned itself into more or less of a slum. She's been trying to sell it for years, no luck, not even at what she's asking now, twelve thousand dollars. I'm sure she'd rent with cries of joy."

What an invaluable woman Lucy is, de Lima said to himself as he so often had occasion to do.

"She doesn't live in it herself?"

"No, she has what in Philadelphia is called an efficiency, near Rittenhouse Square. She teaches at the University of Pennsylvania."

"Can you set all this in train immediately? And you'll need details to pass along to her."

Lucy took a little pad and a pencil out of her pocket.

"His name is John Wright. He's in his fifties, retired because of delicate health. He worked for an insurance company. A responsible, reliable chap. He lost his wife a few years ago. He's planning to write a book, which is why he demands total solitude."

"A book about what?" Lucy asked, wondering if this John Wright was a well-known literary figure who had escaped her notice.

"Nature," de Lima said. "Can you think of anything much duller, to the outsider that is, than writing a book about nature?"

"Offhand, no."

"Good." De Lima beamed. "By the way, this little undertaking has nothing whatever to do with me or the gallery. You know Wright slightly and thought you could accommodate both him and Helena with this rental. And—I don't want to offend you, you model of utter discretion—but *I* am bound by secrecy and so shall bind you to it."

Lucy had been with de Lima for ten years and was a repository of secrets far more loaded than this one seemed to be. She merely smiled, finished her sherry, and got up. "I'll call her at home tonight, I don't know her class schedule."

The more de Lima thought about it the more he liked it. This way, he could keep an eye, as it were, on Swain. By telephone and if necessary in person, and quickly, in case Swain began in some fashion to misbehave. He didn't think Swain would, but always look for the worst and be ready for it.

EIGHT

I don't know what it is about this summer, it's a wrong kind of summer, Johanna thought, an odds-and-ends summer with a hollowness at the center of it.

Ireland had been, for three weeks, a welcome diversion, re-searching "The King of Gillybally." Researching was a loose name for what her job actually consisted of. Producer Jack Feroni ran a tight ship indeed; when the expensive people arrived on the scene with their cameras, they would have in hand every detail they could possibly want. In addition to the story itself, neatly typed and colorfully comprehensive, they would know which of the villagers were most enlightening or enter-taining to interview on camera; which of the two inns to stay at; which pub to drink at; what was the best camera angle for shooting the king's renovated castle on the river Gilly; and at what time of day he was sober enough to defend his takeover of the town. On each assignment, the intensive preproduction work on her part saved quantities of time and more impor-tantly thousands of dollars.

She was no sooner back in New York than Jack said, "Take a day or so to catch your breath and then get your ass to San Francisco."

"I have no home," Johanna mock-mourned.

To comfort her, Jack said, "Think of all those women in Levittown screaming to their dust mops, If only I could get the hell out of here."

She had no answering service at home and while there was a pile of casual messages for her at the office there was nothing bearing the name John Swain. No scribble saying "your father called."

Uncivilized, even outrageous, when you thought about it, so don't think about it. Or you'll start that cycle, that awful down-spiraling May cycle, all over again. She had already, she thought, completely dismissed Sam Hines. After all, she had thrown him out of her apartment; a literal and it turned out final dismissal. If she had been another kind of woman, patient, coaxing, soothing, willing to bend her neck and weather his storm. . .

Oh well.

After San Francisco, she was being driven home, late, from a party in Tarrytown, by Roger Gavin, who was doing his best to make her summer wake up. Stopping for a red light, he twiddled the dial on the dashboard radio.

A curious confluence was presented to her ears.

Sam Hines's "All I Can Say Is Maybe" was playing, his lyric wry, sad, and funny by turns. Because he was lyricist to his own music, the marriage was perfect: the lift and fall and whirl of the tune sad and funny too.

At the end of the song, the disc jockey told them the time, two o'clock, and informed them that they were listening to "Wacky," Station WKKI, Trenton, New Jersey. "And now here's one of our special wacky questions for you. Does anybody out there know how we can get in touch with an artist, a painter, named John Swain?"

At her sharply indrawn breath, Roger asked, "What's the matter, Johanna?"

"Nothing—except I hadn't realized it was so late."

The name Swain in connection with her wouldn't mean anything to Roger. She had told no one about this relationship and had no intention in future of breaking her silence. It wouldn't make, at the outside, a very self-flattering story. And it didn't bear talking about.

Boasting about? "The artist, you know." "How fascinating. Do you see him often?"

On Sunday morning, she got up at a sandy-eyed eight o'clock and called WKKI in Trenton.

She found out that the two o'clock voice belonged to Stanley Parker and was given without hesitation his home phone number. "He gets lots of calls," the girl said. "He has quite a little fan club. People wanting pictures of him and things."

When she rang the number, the phone was picked up and a voice as if at a distance from it shouted, "Damn it, Alice, where the hell are you?" and then, "Sorry, I'd just gone to bed, who's this?"

"I heard you asking last night about John Swain, about getting in touch with him."

"Yes, have you got some information? It's not for me, it's for another party. You didn't say who you are."

"Johanna Landis. I'm a relative of John Swain's."

"Well, then, where does he hang out?"

"I'm not prepared to offer any information until I know what this radio hunt is all about."

"Okay. Give me your name again, spell it please, and your number and I'll have the party get in touch with you and explain it herself." She complied with only a slight flicker of hesitation, added her office address and number, and then said, "Give me her name, if you will."

"Smith." He laughed. "Honest-to-God Smith. First name Alice."

Right away Johanna half regretted this call. Now she would be housebound all day, waiting to hear from the Smith woman. What, in any case, was she expecting to hear? Had she followed this up out of some instinct of protection for him? A man in a Maine town being paged by what sounded like a trashy Jersey radio station—very odd. But then, the three of them had been living in Morristown with her mother's Aunt Ella, when her father had taken his departure. Someone from his past. Or even someone who conceivably wanted to buy a painting of his. No, a picture.

Well, here was an unrivaled opportunity to apply herself to the stack of mail, mostly bills and junk, which she had found jammed into her mailbox when she got back from the Coast. In between Consolidated Edison and Lord & Taylor bills was a white envelope, the name in the left-hand corner Hines.

"Dear Johanna, whenever I call you're not there—or anywhere—so I have been forced to take pen to paper." Nice handwriting, free and forcible. "You have already inspired several possible song titles: 'My Nowhere Girl' or 'If I Don't Reach You Don't Think I'm Not Trying' or 'All Alone by the Telephone'—no, that's been done I believe. Now I have to go back to Paris." Back? Paris? Why? When had he gone before? "Anyway, wherever you are (I must add that to my list of titles) tell me when our two ships do pass and salute each other why you didn't like your tulips and never said a word. In fact, you might write me a line at the Plaza Athénée and explain yourself. Sam."

Tulips? *What* tulips? She tried to discourage a faint rising warmth under her ribs. The only sensible conclusion was that he was confusing her with someone else. But she could—she who had been so haunted for a time by another noncommunication from another man—have the decency to write a short note.

She did it immediately, before she became even more convinced that he was mixing her up with some other female. A temporarily blurred mind, perhaps—weren't there a lot of no-nonsense drugs drifting about the musical world? He hadn't looked it, though. He had looked very much himself, the edges sharp, the eyes clear, the gaze direct and directed.

"Dear Sam, I'm sorry we couldn't connect. I've been in Ireland and then in San Francisco, but after all you are in Paris and apparently were there not so long ago if it's a case of going *back*. Now I hear mutters that my next destination is Japan. Oh well. Johanna." After a pause of her pen, she added, "P.S. What tulips?" She hadn't committed herself to anything beyond mere politeness; he couldn't know what her "oh well" meant. Or might, she corrected, mean.

She got a number of telephone calls late in the morning when people she knew got up from their Sunday feast of sleep, but none from Stanley Parker's party, Alice Smith. At one o'clock Johanna thought, To hell with Alice Smith, and went off with Roger Gavin to a late leisurely lunch at P.J. Clarke's.

He dropped her at her apartment at four. At four-thirty, the doorbell rang. Johanna peered through her eyehole. A girl, a stranger. She opened the door.

"Hello there," said the girl. "I'm Alice Smith. May I come in? I called three times but there was no answer so I thought I'd kill some time and then come around and see. You're Johanna, aren't you?"

Johanna wondered at the informality of dispensing with her last name. "Yes, do come in."

Alice Smith was a small, slight girl, delicately pretty, with a rosy little self-contained mouth, a short straight nose, and limpid, innocent blue eyes. The ribbon holding back her hazel-blond hair, shining and fine as a child's hair, was a blue exactly matching her eyes. She wore a white eyelet-embroidered sleeveless dress and gave the impression of just having come out of a bath, or a bandbox, morning-fresh.

Johanna, studying her without seeming to do so, found herself being studied in turn. Then, "What a pretty apartment," Alice Smith said. She went to one of the casement windows and looked out. "Gardens down there. My, how nice. And right in the middle of New York City. And look a swimming pool on top of that apartment up the street."

Find out what this sweet young thing wanted before offering tea or coffee or a drink. "It was on your behalf that the John Swain question came up on WKKI last night?"

"Yes, he's—the disc jockey—quite a friend of mine." She smiled and Johanna thought, All that's missing is a dimple. "You told him you were a relative of John Swain's."

"Yes—somewhat distant." An understatement in several contexts.

"I'm his"—Alice paused and touched one of the little wings of hair that curved forward over the blue ribbon—"his daughter."

Johanna's heart gave a small crash. "His daughter? Smith?"

"Just between us, because we're each other's family I suppose, John Swain was a man my mother knew before she, well, met my father. My father didn't mind adopting me." Alice had decided it sounded nicer that way.

She looks perfectly sane, Johanna thought in a distress she didn't understand at all, and sounds very sure of herself.

"I suppose you have some proof of this?"

"Why would you want proof?" Clear wide-eyed glance. "I mean, if you're a distant relative and if all I want from you is where I can find Mr. Swain?"

"If you're his daughter how is it you have no idea where he is?"

She smiled again. "He doesn't know about me. I only found out myself a little while ago. About who my real father was, I mean. You may think it's sentimental of me but I feel I must see him. Well, wouldn't anyone? And then last month I found out that he's a famous *artist*. I'm so proud of him. How, exactly, are you related to him?"

"Second cousin once removed."

"It's so nice, such fun to find a sort of new family of my own. Let's stand in front of your mirror and see if we look like each other."

Churlish to refuse such a simple request. "We don't, do we," Alice said. "Maybe our eyebrows . . . you must have a picture of him around?"

"No, I haven't." Something about Johanna's voice, a projected warning chill, reached her guest. "Well, then, if you'll just give me his address."

Without at the moment examining her motives, Johanna said, "He's in Europe, I have no idea where and for how long. He did have a place, rented. In Litchfield, Connecticut, but he gave that up when he went abroad in May. We don't correspond, so . . ." She let the trailing off signify that this piece of information was complete, and finished.

Alice sighed. "Oh, my. And I had such high hopes of you. I suppose I'll just have to keep looking and looking. Like that song, 'Little Girl Blue.' I've written the National Gallery in London—maybe they'll know where he is, but they haven't answered yet though it's been three weeks."

A silence fell. Johanna let it lie there. She found herself to her horror mentally commanding. And now would you mind taking yourself off, you blue-ribbon bitch. *Bitch?* Why? Plain ugly jealousy?

She herself, just seeing his signature on a canvas, had felt that she had at last to see him. Wouldn't anyone? Wouldn't Alice?

Wouldn't Alice probably like a little of the reflected glow of the artist's growing reputation and the reflected green of the artist's money? Now I am the one, Johanna told herself firmly, who qualifies for the label bitch.

"Well, at least *we've* gotten to know each other," Alice said as if trying to find some reward for her trouble in coming here. "I'll give you my address and phone number in New Jersey, shall I? And then if you want to get in touch with me or whatever . . . And he might send you a postcard from somewhere, you could let me know. Or if he gets back. Please."

"Of course." Johanna got out her address book and took down the unwanted information.

". . . and during the week I'm at Berlin's Department Store in Trenton, you'll want that too. I'm the president's Girl Friday."

Bully for you. "That's nice. I'd like to offer you something but"—eyes going to the clock—"I'm running a bit late and I must dress and dash out of here."

"I must too. Stanley will be dying for his dinner." She gave Johanna a roguish look.

Stanley? Oh. Talk about having a friend at court. One's partner having the facilities of a radio station at his disposal.

"Byebye then till our next get-together." Alice left and treated herself to a taxi to Penn Station, where she would get her train to Trenton. She thought about Johanna Landis. Nasty thing in a way. She looked as though she could be very nice to other people but not to me. Went to some snob college I suppose. And her apartment is . . . and here I thought ours was so nice. We should have a bookcase, though books get so dusty. I'll probably never hear another peep from her, but now anyway I know where to find her.

At dinner, she said to Stanley, "Seeing that you landed her—that's funny, landed Landis—will you try again in a week or so?"

Matt Cummings had long since worn out his welcome at Joe Rainey's and was staying at the New York apartment of friends who had gone to France for a month. The only requirements, they told him, were that he water their plants—thirty-five of them—and walk their two poodles three times a day.

Goddamned gardener, that's what I am, Matt thought as at three in the morning he watered the plants. He had forgotten all about them for four days and they looked a bit ailing.

Another job interview the day before had turned out zero: assistant editor on the trade publication *Supermarket Scope.* Matt told the editor that he had had heavy experience actually managing supermarkets, and had written himself letters of recommendation from A & P, Shop-rite, and Food Fair. The editor gave him a typed list of twenty appalling questions to answer, on things like traffic flow, shelving options, loss leaders, and the Falk theory of meat cutting and display. Trying desperately to write something, anything, with the pen shaking in his fingers, he knew by question number five that the only thing to do was to lay down the pen and get the hell out.

Face red with rage and frustration, explanation which tried to sound busy and crisp, "Another appointment, hadn't figured on the long wait to get in to see you—be back later to finish filling out your questionnaire"—and a glance at his wrist where his watch should be. He kept forgetting that he had pawned his watch.

Ordinarily he kept the radio tuned, loud, to Station WQXR, but he was in no mood for classical music. Serenity, beauty, and accomplishment meeting the ear, although some of the poor bastards had had a terrible time: early death, poverty, blindness. But they'd made a mark and they would never die.

Dying. Matt thought. Not a bad idea. But not yet. Sooner or later something will break. If I don't, waiting for it.

Oh Maggie. . . .

The howling, furious music from some Jersey station was just right for the way he felt. Nightmare music, nightmare words. "I don't like it down here in hell, baby, come and cool me off, willya?"

The disc jockey came on with a pitch for a chain of bowling alleys. Then, "Here's another wacky question for you night owls. Anybody know where the famous artist John Swain hangs out? Call this number if you can give me a clue."

Matt called the number. The jockey answered. "Is there any reward, monetary reward, for information on John Swain?" Matt asked.

"No. Just," with a snicker, "the reward of feeling you have done a good turn for another human being."

Go ahead, boil over.

"All right, I can tell you where John Swain is. Right now he's in six pieces in a cook pot set before the king of the little-known Third World country of Tobamba. He and his aides will consume Swain as soon as their wine is properly chilled to wash him down with."

"Thanks a lot, buster. You crazy or something?" Stanley Parker said, and hung up.

Part 2

ONE

Excerpt from Coming Events Calendar, *Art Today* magazine:

In late September, the prestigious de Lima Gallery will
put on a major retrospective of the work of John Swain
(exact date still to be announced). In the estimation of
many museum curators and private collectors, Swain is
joining the small imperishable company of the greats. To
review his past-to-present rise for those who are not
familiar with it, Swain began as an art instructor at St.
Elizabeth's Academy in Morristown, New Jersey. He left
this post to fling himself into the uncertain seas of luck
and talent and . . .

"Good heavens," de Lima said when he got his advance
copy of the magazine. He had dictated the publicity release to
Lucy and the *Art Today* writer had used all the bones of it and
added a good deal of colorful flesh. "Fling himself into the
uncertain seas . . ." Rather uncomfortably right on the nose.
But, perhaps a good thing. It might be picked up in the report
of his death as an eerie verbal coincidence.

He was, he told himself because he couldn't tell anyone else,
all butterflies inside, flocks of them beating their wings delicately against his pulses and nerve ends. In mid-September, his
trucker with his forty-foot moving van returned from Bride's

Bay, delivering the thirty-one canvases to a warehouse
de Lima owned in SoHo. An armed guard, who didn't look
armed and didn't wear a guard's uniform, lived there, along
with two Doberman pinschers. De Lima was very much afraid
of the pinschers and telephoned to have them chained up
before he arrived to take a peek at Swain's tremendous six-
month outpouring of everything he had. In awe and glee, de
Lima hugged himself.

Choose, say, just six of the thirty-one for the retrospective,
to hang along with the canvases borrowed back from museums and private collections. Then, perhaps in January, stage
a major show of new work. A bombshell flung up from an unmarked grave in the depths of the Atlantic Ocean.

"Don't tell me when the event will take place," he had said
to Swain in a recent telephone conversation. "I wouldn't be
able to sleep. You *are* a strong swimmer, are you not?"

But he couldn't keep himself from watching the weather
reports on television. Lying in his comfortable bed, with its
Irish linen sheets and light blanket woven of cashmere, he
thought with horror of the stormy ocean. Depths upon dark
invisible depths beneath one's poor vulnerable human body,
unseen things perhaps lurking in them, monsters who might
suddenly seize a limb and remove it. The only water he was not
terrified in was of the expensive resort variety. And then no
deeper than his waist, and brilliantly clear so that you could
see every sand ripple on the bottom, hastening to the shore if
even a tiny crab appeared to one's nervous vision. But Swain
. . . waves, mountains, seething with power, lifting their awful
walls behind you and ahead of you. His stomach would drop
away, the bed would seem to surge under him, and de Lima on
many a night got up and gave himself either a dose of scotch
or a sleeping pill.

The storm wasn't of the apocalyptic, record-book variety
but it was bad enough and it would have to do. He had lived in
limbo long enough and felt he couldn't stand it one day
longer.

It would of course have been simpler just to get out of the
Star on the seaward side of Pascoe Island and get into
Maggie's waiting Star. But, by his calculations (although he

acknowledged to himself that he was a casual sailor, not an expert) to get a good bashing against the sea-facing rocks the boat would first have to be carried some distance. What was also wanted was a forlorn waterlogged look.

And if he left it to its own devices at the edge of the island, the contrary craft might nose in under an overhanging rock and press its bow into some sort of securing cleft and be found perfectly dry, safe, and seaworthy during the search for John Swain. Which wouldn't do at all.

It was a little after four in the afternoon but it looked much later in the dark lightning-split sky. The rain poured and hissed on the hilled and valleyed water. The island was roughly an eighth of a mile astern. He saw the sentence in the newspapers, "Swept overboard while . . ."

Now.

The thing was to work with the water, work with the waves and not against them. You are not trying to push me under, cut off my air, you are trying to help me, carry me where I want to go. He didn't use his fast efficient crawl, but breast-stroked strongly, head above water most of the time, coasting downward, stroking upward.

Christ, how could an eighth of a mile be so vast a distance? Six hundred and sixty feet, or read it in yards, that sounded shorter. Two hundred and twenty yards.

Bad moment when he thought he was going to be thrown hard against the rock face. He threw himself backward and took the shock with his feet and legs. He turned his head to his left and saw Maggie's Star, without lights, coming to him.

One arm braced about the mast, she reached down and helped him scramble aboard. "Thank God, darling. It's getting worse too, isn't that nice?" He felt her trembling. Maggie trembling? Never before in his experience.

In the unlikely event that anyone had spotted her boat, leaving the dock in the peak of the storm, and reported it later, she had prepared to handle that with, "I was worried about him, he'd been depressed and drinking. I went out to look for him but then turned back—hopeless out there."

It was a short sail to the cove. She poled the Star into the boathouse, the hinged roof of which was now open to accommodate the mast. Inside, there was a wide slip for the two boats and on right and left raised boardwalks and lockers for gear. Even open, the slant of the roof kept the boardwalks dry. She pulled closed the heavy, half-rotted seaward door. Now, except to the house on the hill, Swain's house, they were invisible.

She wasted no time in discussions of his adventure. She opened a locker and took out a bottle of scotch and two glasses and poured him a stiff drink while she got out a heavy towel and a small suitcase. Their only light was a candle in a dusty Ballantine beer bottle. Swain disposed of his scotch in two gulps. Now it was he who was trembling. No, shivering. Although the September sea had not been all that cold.

He took off his bathing trunks and put on dry clothes from the skin out. Not John Swain clothes, not the black jersey and corduroys. A flannel suit in medium condition which Maggie had picked up several weeks before at a yard sale, a white oxford cloth shirt, an undistinguished tie, brown socks, and brown brogues she had found in his closet, a mouse making its home in one of them. Then the wig, a dull brown, a little long but not fashionably so. just the effect that he hadn't quite gotten around to a needed haircut. "I wonder if I should try a little suggestion of dandruff in it," she had mused when she bought it. "White cornmeal . . ." "No dandruff," said Swain. Smoke-tinted glasses. "At night?" Swain had asked. "Why?" "You have an eye condition which needs protection even from night lights." And now with a little rouge on the tip of her forefinger she reddened the rims of his eyes over and under. "As you well know, darling, your eyes are in a way your signature. Never, *never* appear without your glasses. I bought you four different colors."

She had rented a car several days ago from the place she used three or four times a year when she went off to visit friends; Lockett's in Tinkertown. It was in the barn. They parted at the dock. Swain made a detour and went up through the cover of the pines and she climbed the open grassy hill. They met again in the barn. It was now almost completely dark and still raining heavily.

"Remember, back roads until past Tinkertown." Swain would remember; he had a map in his head. "Don't, for God's sake, call me when you get there. There may be police around, reporters, all hell breaking loose. I'll be in touch with you when it's safe.''

They held each other in a way new to them, cherishingly. Then, using only parking lights, Swain started the car and drove out of the barn.

He was to leave the Toyota at Logan Airport in Boston, where Lockett's had an office, and go to a motel near the airport. In the morning, de Lima, who would spend his night in superior comfort at the Ritz-Carlton, would pick him up at his motel and drive him to Seashell Park.

Maggie waited an hour before going to the telephone in her apartment. She called both the police and the Coast Guard and gave her report in a voice of barely controlled panic.

John Swain, she said, had gone out at three-thirty, intending a short sail to clear his head. Now here it was after seven and he wasn't back yet. She had thought he might have sailed in to shore to escape the storm, somewhere near, up or down the coast; he had done that before on occasion when he was caught short by the weather. She had waited for the phone call saying all was well, but it hadn't come. He might still be perfectly all right, having a drink at somebody's house, and had just forgotten to call her, but she hadn't dared to wait any longer before notifying the authorities.

"Damned fool," said the chief of police, and sighed. "Oh, well. Artists.''

"That radio is going to drive me mad," Swain said on Saturday morning an hour after they started the long rainy drive from Boston to New Jersey. They were not ensconced in de Lima's Bentley, but in a rented buff-colored Chevrolet which nobody would look at twice.

"You ought soon to be hitting the airwaves with a crash," de Lima said. "We wouldn't want to miss that.''

He had given Swain a concentrated head-to-foot examination when he picked him up at the motel. "Mmmm. You look very nearly commonplace. But grow a mustache, immediately. It will help draw attention from your nose. It is too bad about your nose.''

"I hate mustaches.''

"You're not you anymore, dear fellow. John Wright has

always yearned for a mustache. No beard, though, you might go back to looking noticeable again.''

Between radio news breaks, de Lima proffered advices that were very close to commands. ''Don't go getting any showy art books from the library, if there is a library in that benighted town. Don't out of curiosity turn up at any possible local-nobody openings in nearby towns, or arts-and-crafts fairs, or anything of that nature. Don't make an acquaintance of anyone who has anything at all to do with art, even if it's only painting by numbers. Most importantly, do not dare under any circumstances to take brush or pencil in hand. You are a retired man in delicate health, all you know about is insurance. If you must produce a hobby in addition to your literary work, say you are devoted to crossword puzzles.''

Listening, Swain felt light-headed and unreal. Well.

He was unreal.

His months, weeks, days throbbing with work and excitement had swept him into September. He had given very little thought to the other life after that. He was aware of an immense fatigue of flesh and spirit, and, for the moment, of being painted out. Resting for a while, not thinking of anything at all, might be pleasant.

A few miles south of Fall River, the Boston station news announcer with his broad *a* finished a bulletin on a fire in a parking garage on Tremont Street. ''And, this just in. According to unconfirmed reports, noted American artist John Swain may have lost his life in a boating accident in a heavy storm yesterday off Bride's Bay, Maine. The Coast Guard has found his boat, empty and damaged, on the rocky shore of Pascoe Island. A sea and air hunt continues. It is not known whether Swain kept a life raft in his boat but little hope for his survival is held out. In Washington, Republican Senator Herbert Green of Michigan has proposed that the highway speed limit of his state should be . . .'' Swain snapped the radio off.

''There you go, John,'' said de Lima. He was pale under his olive coloring and there were delicate little beads on his high rounded forehead. ''Early as it is, you might reach into the glove compartment and get out my flask. We will pull off the road at the first opportunity and have a mourning drink at your private wake.''

Lifting the flask, which was amiably equipped on top with two sterling silver jiggers, he said, "The holy progression—marc, cognac, armagnac. This is armagnac. Thirty years old. Although at the moment your taste buds may understandably be a bit dead . . ." He stopped in mid sip. "Sorry, John. And in this connection I must tell you that you are not to be disappointed if the coverage of your death, television, radio, newspapers, is a bit muted. It's what one would expect in our uncivilized country. It would be different if this were France. And *quite* different here, if you, wiped out, were a professional football player—or better still, Johnny Carson."

TWO

Swain in spite of de Lima's warning drew a reasonably splashy press.

He was front page in the New York *Times* (lower right-hand corner): "American Artist John Swain Appears Lost in Storm at Sea." The following day the *Times's* art critic devoted half a page to his life and work and death. There were three reproductions of his paintings which in black and white looked merely like blurs, or clouds. ". . . his door was just swinging wide open when Swain met his tragic death off Bride's Bay, Maine. On September 30, the de Lima Gallery will stage a major retrospective of his work, with paintings on loan from many of the world's great museums, and from private collections. There will also be six new works complete before his death, of which I found 'Number Seventy-one' overpowering in its solemn, surging tonalities."

The news weeklies were generous with their space. But then, it was a good story. The little *Star* in the raging water, the tall shabby white house on the hill looking down on its cove, the man after his long struggle approaching the peak of his personal mountain: a resounding crash of recognition. UBC had a network affiliate in Portland and a camera crew arrived on the scene. The artist's tenant, Mrs. Lind, allowed interior shots of Swain's house as he had left it that fatal afternoon. A sketchbook flopped over the arm of his chair, which when

72

losely examined by the lens showed delightful mists of color, ignettes for pictures which would now never be swept over anvas. His half-full coffee mug on a windowsill, a piece of ound steak for his dinner waiting raw on a plate on the :itchen counter. On the mantelpiece, a rusty old coffee can ull of brushes. And in the barn, an immense canvas begun, he paint still wet, as one crudely daring fingertip found. Then here was a run-through of his pictures, ten of them, using :olor transparencies supplied by the de Lima Gallery.

No, de Lima told the *Times* and the news weeklies, the net-vorks, and the art publications, he had no photograph of Swain. Swain, like members of some religious sects or obscure iative tribes, disliked having his picture taken. "Borrowing rom Wren and his St. Paul's," de Lima said, "he had the eeling that his work was the only true picture of Swain the nan."

The air-sea hunt had been abandoned after forty-eight hours. The Star with its pathetic broken mast was towed to shore and put back in the boathouse; it was not damaged beyond repair and the Coast Guard thought the heirs might want it if only for reasons of sentiment.

Heirs? The press was puzzled about this matter. It was unclear at the moment who the heir or heirs were. This in-formation might have to wait until the will went to probate. "Somebody's going to make a potful from here on in," said an *Art Today* man to an ART*news* man.

In its mysterious all-knowing way, the *Times* in its coverage of the story produced Swain's wife and daughter, Johanna. "After a divorce in 1957, Mrs. Swain married Stephen Landis, a partner in the Wall Street firm of Landis and Landis."

De Lima faultlessly maintained his mien of discreet gloom, of trying to bear a heavy weight as best he could. He was gratified to get telephone calls from all over the world. Lily Patchester's call was typical of many. "But he *did* leave some work behind! Oh, thank God. D'you know, I cried when I heard? I'll be over for the show. Don't you dare part with a single one until I get there." Japan on the line, Rio de Janeiro, Montreal. Yes, frightful, appalling. One of the worst shocks of his lifetime. He still could not believe that that vital man, overflowing with power and, yes, with genius, was dead. His "that magnificent flame quenched in the sea" was an epitaph widely quoted.

To him, de Lima, a profound personal loss as well. They had been not only professional associates but friends for more than thirteen years; indeed, he might be said to have discovered Swain. "But that's in a way like saying you discovered the World Trade Center on the New York skyline."

Johanna having, what with the summer's working travels, only picked up bits and pieces of her social life here and there, proposed to gather some friends around her for a small party on Sunday evening.

She got up Saturday morning to begin her arrangements. Outside errands first; people would be sleeping late. Not an addict of supermarkets, she started her shopping at Vane's, a luxurious little store around the corner from her apartment. She had been on expense account most of the summer and was well in funds.

Dinner would have to be buffet; her round table only seated six at a pinch and she had roughly twelve people in mind. Serve something simple, which could be managed on laps and little tables. Lobster Newburg, a salad, a bowl of fresh fruit in kirsch, sesame breadsticks, an Italian rum cake which she could pick up at Fanti's on Third Avenue. Leaving her paper bags at Vane's to be collected later, she walked to Fanti's. A light rain was falling, fresh against the skin, combing, she thought gratefully, all that gook out of the air.

At Fanti's, the radio behind the counter was on, low. An aria concluded, and the announcer said, "And now from the wires of the Associated Press, the news at eleven."

"Would you happen to have a rum cake on the premises?" Johanna asked Mr. Fanti, whose shop she had been visiting for several years.

". . . oil tanker in a collision with a merchant vessel in the Indian Ocean . . ."

"Yes. Fresh this morning. Half or whole this time?"

". . . internationally known American artist John Swain in reports as yet unconfirmed is believed to have lost his life yesterday when his sailboat was caught in a storm off the coast of Bride's Bay, Maine. The air and sea hunt . . ."

"Half or whole?"

He looked with alarm at his customer on the other side of the glass bakery case. "Are you all right?"

She moved down a few feet to grip the edge of the counter.

". . . no progress has been made in the teachers' strike in Chicago. Both sides remain far away from an agreement. The principal stumbling block is . . ."

"Half or whole rum cake, Miss Landis?"

"Oh. Whole." She watched without seeing him putting the cake tenderly into its white box and tying the box with string. She picked up the box and started for the door. He called after her, "Did you want to pay for that or would you like to open a charge, Miss Landis?"

"I'm sorry—thinking of something else—" She dug clumsily in her handbag, got out her wallet, gave him a ten-dollar bill and while she was waiting for the change saw the bakery tilt and felt that its delightful fragrance might any second now make her ill.

"Enjoy it. Are you sure you're all right?"

"Yes."

Unconfirmed reports. He could have swum to some shore. And weren't there hundreds of little islands off the coast of Maine? She had seen one of them from his window. But, could he swim? Who unable to swim would take a boat out into the Atlantic? They'd find him soon sitting on some rock, patiently waiting to be picked up. Patiently? Not that man, not John Swain.

Sea and air hunt. Coast Guard helicopters flying low, men with binoculars, maybe sighting him through them right now.

She was vaguely surprised to find herself in her apartment. She couldn't remember coming up the hill from Lexington, crossing the lobby, waiting for one of the two elevators, getting into it, getting out at the right floor, unlocking her door.

And she had forgotten to pick up the two paper bags full of her dinner makings. For the party.

She took off her raincoat and stood looking at it. Was it too wet to put in the closet? Hang it over the bathtub, on the shower rail. Yes, do that.

How long could you stand in the center of your room with a wet raincoat over your arm?

The doorbell rang. It must be the boy from Vane's delivering her overlooked groceries. She let the raincoat fall to the floor and stood staring for a moment toward the door.

Walking slowly over the polished parquet floor, as though she were very old and a slip might end up in a broken hip, she opened the door. Sam Hines stood outside, raindrops on his dark hair. He came in without invitation.

"I heard just a little while ago, Johanna. I called but there was no answer. I thought you might be out on Saturday-morning errands. I thought you oughtn't to be alone right now. I didn't know if you would or wouldn't be alone."

He looked at her face, and the raincoat on the floor. He took her hand. "You heard?"

"While I was buying a rum cake, yes. Just now. Just a few minutes ago. Unconfirmed report."

"I talked to Maggie half an hour ago. She hadn't any sort of hope left." Cruel kindness, or kind cruelty, he wasn't sure which, but it had to be said. She was only—naturally, inevitably—putting off the blow. It would be that much worse when the blow connected with the cringing flesh and bone.

"As I was telling myself before your car bumped into me," Johanna said in a pale cool voice, not her voice at all, "you can't lose what you've never had. But it is . . . awful. Isn't it awful?" She began to tremble.

He dropped her hand, took off his raincoat, picked hers up off the floor, and went into the bathroom with them. Over his shoulder, he asked, "Did he ever get in touch with you?"

"No."

"Christ."

In a world that had gone strange for the time, it didn't seem particularly odd that he was here, now, with her. He was indelibly connected with woe, with her father, with tears, with bleak disappointment, and somewhere mixed up in the middle of all that, with rescue.

She heard him, as though this apartment was his and not hers, opening cabinet doors in the kitchen, a rattle of bottles, glass clinking against glass. He came in with brandy for her and for him, put down the little balloon glasses, took her by the shoulders and pushed her gently down against the stack of pillows in the corner of her bed, covered by day in tangerine velvet. He retrieved the glasses, sat down beside her, and became in a manner quite unlike him voluble.

"If you don't want to know now, you'll want to know later. He left the house around three. The storm began to let loose an hour later. Maggie will never forgive herself because she waited until seven to call the police and the Coast Guard but she thought he'd pulled in somewhere and was drying off and would soon be in touch with her. That had happened before. He was happy and well, there's apparently no possibility of suicide. His show opens here at the end of the month, a whopper, a retrospective, the real beginning, she said, of his fireworks."

"Was she . . . how was she?" Johanna asked. How was the woman loved, or needed, or both, by her father—the one who of the two of them could truly be called bereaved?

"Bad—all mixed up—talking in jerks. I had to sort it out. I told her to come down and stay with me and she said she might when she learned how to move a hand or foot again. There were people there, the press I suppose, she couldn't talk long. A lot of noise, voices, around her. Drink your brandy, Johanna." She drank half of it, sip by slow sip. It helped the trembling. "And just to clear us up. I gather from your note that you never got mine, the day after you threw me out of here. A deed well done, I may add. I was going away, Paris, and I wrote to apologize, with flowers. The flowers you can do without but when I realized that all this time you thought I'd just kicked you in the teeth and called it a day, I damn near collapsed."

He swallowed some of his own brandy, took a gauging look at her face, and talked on. "I thought television research was just working away in a room painted gray, with computers to the left of you and ranks of telephones to the right of you—'Hello there, did you watch "Archie Bunker" last night?' But when I called, you were always somewhere else. Was it the North Pole last time? I should have left my name but you have a secretary or whatever who always demands, Is this *urgent?* I quail and say no. I could hardly have dictated a message to her as follows, Dear Johanna, please forgive me, I am sorry from the soles of my feet up. Will you? Do you, now?"

"Yes, of course." She was beginning to feel a little steadier. Was it the first, brutal shock wearing off, or was it his presence? She found herself really seeing him for perhaps the first time. Something Gallic about the long bony face, the confident nose, the flexible knowing mouth. Did one of his dark eyebrows ride a little higher than the other by birth or was that the way he arranged his face? He gave an engaging, vital impression of awareness and response.

The doorbell rang again. "I'll go," he said, "though I don't suppose reporters—" He opened the door. "Thanks, put them in the kitchen," and Johanna heard from around the corner of the L-shaped room the rustle of paper bags and the clink of coins. "Your groceries," Sam said, coming back to her.

"I was going to give a party. Sunday. I don't think after all I will."

"Does everyone you know know about Swain? Maybe a little sympathy wouldn't come amiss."

"No one knows," Johanna said. "No one but you. You can probably understand why, having been on the scene of the great reunion."

"Yes. Well, I'm not going to leave you alone here with nothing to look at but the rain coming down. Put on a dry coat and I'll take you to lunch. You don't have to talk at all, I'll talk enough for both. I have to go to Nyack this afternoon but we've got until three."

In spite of the return from the void, there was still the feeling of unreality, of being jolted out of place and time. But, move. Go into the bathroom. Hair. Face. A little lipstick? Was her jersey pants suit all right? Yes, entirely suitable, black. Perhaps a scarf around the neck to do something more about the stark face? White? No. Salmon, or the checked lavender? No scarf. Too much trouble. *What did it feel like, to drown?* Nails, clean. Earrings. The first to hand, on the edge of the basin from last night. It was disgraceful of her not to cry. But, too cold and numbed for crying. Wet shoes to be changed. Button your coat. Lunch. Sam Hines.

THREE

God, what a dismal place, Swain thought on waking to his third full day in Seashell Park.

Helena Coe's bedroom had too much alien female atmosphere for him: frills on the lampshades, eyelet-embroidered dressing-table skirt, an unnerving triple-mirror screen in one corner, a faded rug over which giant roses sprawled. Instead he took the one guest room with a window looking out on the screened front porch. It was small and crowded with its double bed, large blue-painted chest of drawers, and armchair with a table and reading lamp.

For the third day in a row, the rain poured down. There was no place so damp-through soaking-*wet*, he thought, as a place by the sea whose only reason for existence was blue skies and hot sunlight. Unlike the Maine coast, where you expected the worst and got it, in houses built for the worst.

He was not only not himself anymore, he had none of his familiar clothing to put on as known and comforting outer skins. De Lima had selected his retired-insurance-man wardrobe for him, some of it new from Macy's and some of it picked up at secondhand stores. United Parcel had delivered the boxes yesterday. He never wore pajamas to sleep in, but wore them with irritation, now. ("Whatever *you* are used to doing, have *him* do the opposite," de Lima had counseled, or

79

ordered. "Up to and including wearing pajamas in bed, you unclothed savage.")

And, "*Put on your wig the instant you get out of bed,*" said the voice of his mentor in his ear. "*In fact, it would be wiser if you slept in it.*" "*I will not sleep in a wig.*" "*Then let us hope you will not be taken ill in the night, and need help, and be found with your persona down.*" He took the wig from the top right-hand dresser drawer and pulled it on; already he hated the thing. Because of the closely securing band inside, it felt like pulling on a headache.

Thank God that on Maggie's first visit she would dye his hair and cut it to match the style of this burdensome accessory. It hadn't been done before he took out his boat in case his storm didn't deliver, but instead freaked itself out to sea, leaving him John Swain, and not John Wright, until the next promising storm.

From the closet he took a wool bathrobe, one of the secondhand items, in a color he hated, maroon. The new fake-leather slippers made a depressing elderly slap-slap on the linoleum floor as he went through the small living room to the kitchen. Helena Coe appeared to be careful with her pennies outside her own bedroom door: the pattern was worn off the linoleum in places, and where it remained it set Swain's teeth on edge, interlocking circles and squares in a poisonous green and dull orange.

The kitchen was contrarily larger than it needed to be but cluttered without plan or purpose. De Lima, glancing around at the ironing board leaning against the wall, the battered dining table with mismatched chairs, the aged gas stove, and the tan curtains patterned with letters of the alphabet, had said, "Well, you're not one to surround yourself with luxuries, you'll be perfectly at home here."

He made coffee and sat down at the table to drink it. "A man of your type would probably eat cold cereal for breakfast. Cornflakes. Yes, cornflakes—I'm told there are barbarous people, in places like this, who drop in on other people for morning coffee and you would best be discovered crunching your bowlful." Here Swain drew the line. Coffee was his breakfast and always would be.

The window beside the table looked out on a small sandy-bare yard with a clothes pole as its sole ornament. Beyond it were the backs of modest houses, very close together, built in the style Swain called Early Nineteen-Nothing. Anonymous houses, desolate in the rain, which he supposed in summer swarmed with shrieking children and echoed with the *whish* of beer cans being opened.

Outside the kitchen door there was a small deck with steps leading down to the yard. To climb up to the deck, you had to pass the window. Starting on his second cup of coffee, Swain looked through the glass into the face of a woman, her nose pressed shamelessly against it. Oh God, too late to hide, run, no one at home, sorry. She knocked at the door and then without ceremony opened it.

"Hi there, neighbor!" she cried. "I've brought you some of my cinnamon buns, fresh-baked. As a sort of housewarming present. I thought it was high time we got acquainted."

She was a short thick woman with a snarled little pink, pug face. She wore a loose printed garment buttoned down the front and tan leather strap sandals. Her hair dye was in various stages of bright gold, orange-amber, and at the parting a grayed brown. In her fifties, Swain judged, and went on to think uncharitably, But she looks as though she's always been in her fifties.

"I'll just pop them in the oven to warm them up for you."

"Thanks, no, I've had my breakfast," Swain protested. "Cornflakes."

"They wouldn't hold body and soul together." She pulled open the oven door and lit the pilot light with a match from a book in her pocket. "I wouldn't say no to sitting down and having one with you. Rainy day like this, it's nice to have company. I'd have been over sooner but I only got back late yesterday from visiting my sister in Trenton. Funny Miss Coe wouldn't have cleaned out this oven for you. It's all cracked-looking black and spills inside. I'll dash over sometime and do it for you with Oven-Off. My name is Garble, Ada Garble. And you're Mr. Wright. Shall we start off with John and Ada? Miss Coe told me about you and I thought how nice it would be to have a neighbor in this dreary hole, well, dreary in the off-season I mean."

While the buns heated, she allowed herself a good thorough

look at him. She wondered what his eyes were like. "Dark
glasses?" she inquired. "Raining like this?"

"An eye infection. Chronic."

"Oh. Too bad." Her gaze went to the third finger of his left
hand, on which de Lima had forced a gold wedding ring.
("Men of your style, or lack of it, wear wedding rings.") She
said in a suitably mournful tone, "Your wife, Miss Coe
said . . ."

"Yes. Passed on." For a moment he felt a vague pleasure in
this imposture; he had unerringly hit on the correct phrase
without even a rehearsal.

"Oh dear, that's the way it is, isn't it. So did Mr. Garble.
He was in large appliances."

A picture appeared in Swain's head of Mr. Garble accident-
ally trapped and expiring inside one of his refrigerators or
freezers. He didn't dare smile but the creases on either side of
his mouth deepened.

"They ought to be ready now." She got two plates from the
cabinet over the sink and served the buns.

There was nothing for it but to eat them. Something, Swain
thought, has to be done about this woman. He unwillingly dis
cerned that Mrs. Garble might even at this stage have remotely
stirring, waking ideas about him. This poor lonely man next
door, a widower and she a widow. Jesus Christ, Swain said to
himself: not in this case a blasphemy but a kind of prayer.

As she chewed her bun, her eyes seemed to be trying to
pierce their way through his dark glasses. "Now, who do you
remind me of?" she mused. "Maybe, from our old days, a
movie star? I'll have to think about it. You couldn't take off
your glasses for just a second?"

Impossible to refuse. Swain did, narrowing his eyes as if the
light hurt them so that she got only a glimmer of hazel. "Oh
dear, I see, all red around the rims, poor man. Have you tried
a little boric acid and warm water?"

"I have my own special salve. Which reminds me I must go
and do my morning massage with it."

"Oh well, I'll be off then. As a welcome, I thought I'd ask
you to come over for dinner tonight. Nothing fancy, just the
two of us. I'll roast a nice little chicken."

"Thanks very much but social life is out for me, for a

while," Swain said. "I've got to work on my book day and
night."

"*Book.*" Her eyes widened. "A book about what?"

"Nature. Flowers and birds and . . . shells and things." Yes,
the book would have to be heavy on shells. How else to explain to her the long walks on the beach, which at this point, in
this place, seemed to him the only means of saving his future
sanity.

"You must autograph a copy for me when it gets into
print." She got up from the table and gave him an ominously
sweet smile. "It's nice meeting you. It's nice having a neighbor
even if he's too busy for you right now."

He didn't know how long he would continue to obey ninety-
nine of de Lima's hundred commandments, but this morning
he did get out the umbrella for his walk on the beach. "You
are in delicate health, never be seen in the rain without an umbrella. This piece of equipment also suggests intense respecta-
bility."

Holding it over his head took a good deal of the zest and
speed out of walking. And the slowed pace gave him time to
think, for which he was not grateful. He was dead now, John
Swain was dead. Who would mourn him? Perhaps a few of his
summer school students, especially the middle-aged ladies. An
old friend or two, but he had long since fallen out of touch
with his friends. Certainly not his ex-wife, Chloe.

Johanna. His mental eye flinched away from her. "*I was
just passing by on my way to Jonesport and for some reason I
couldn't not . . .*" The sight of her face at his cruel and necessary rejection had burned itself into his memory. She was the
only really injured party in this game.

If, that is, she gave a damn. If, marching with shoulders
squared out of his house, she hadn't said, Well, to hell with
him. The news of his death was bound to be something of a
shock, though, even if a minor one quickly gotten over. It was
a Hobson's choice: bad to think of her getting over a minor
shock, bad to think of her pierced, tears on her face. Awful
thing to do to your own daughter, your only child. Awful.
Awful.

He welcomed the unpleasant diversion of a large ugly dog

advancing on him with an unfriendly growl. "Go home, you nasty brute!" Swain ordered, brandishing his umbrella. The dog showed his teeth, hesitated, and then looking malevolently over his shoulder loped off up the beach.

Crossing the broad empty boardwalk, Swain left the flat gray sea behind him. He walked five dismally house-lined blocks to the grocery and liquor store, McHenry's, which also sold newspapers and periodicals. He bought *Time* magazine, dated today, a publication in which he had never invested before. Probably nothing about him in this issue, his drowning too late for their presses, but he couldn't wait to get home and inspect the pages. Yes, by God, there he was, two paragraphs of him.

" . . . 'that magnificent flame quenched in the sea' is the way Adrian de Lima, Swain's agent and dealer, puts it." A brief verbal picture of the storm, the heeled-over-boat with its crippled mast, the canvas in the barn just started on. And then a rather rushed summary of his work: ". . . a nerve-wracking beauty underneath the soft floating bloom of color. What unseen danger lies here? Death, or hell, or nuclear destruction? Swain hangs in museums in . . ." At the end, a preview of the retrospective to open at the de Lima Gallery on September 30: "Six new Swains will also be on display. Hold your hats and watch while the prices soar."

FOUR

After an entirely sleepless night on Saturday, Johanna fell into bed in exhaustion at eight-thirty Sunday night. She jolted herself awake shortly afterward, from the depths of an unhappy dream. She was trying to walk up to the door of her father's house and couldn't reach it because great waves were dashing against it, then retreating to surge against her. She heard her own convulsive, drowning sound.

No. It had been a sunlit day in May. She remembered the shine of the buttercups, and the net curtain which, drifting out the window, reminded her of an Andrew Wyeth picture. And the voice—

A ripple of starled nerves took her from head to foot.

It hadn't come back until now. It had been incomprehensible then.

A woman's voice from somewhere above. *"Time to get back to work, darling, seeing that you have only what? five or so months on this earth left."*

What were the words really saying? What could she have meant? An awful, hidden disease, some kind of death sentence pronounced by a doctor? There had been a touch of merriment in the warm exotic voice. Surely you wouldn't make a joke of a lover's certified doom?

She had been reasonably accurate. His remaining life-span turned out to be the better part of five months.

But how would they know, he and she, in May, about a calamitous and for him final storm off Bride's Bay in mid-September?

In her weary confusion, she committed what she later considered to be a severe gaffe. Without stopping to think about it, she got out of bed and dialed Sam Hines's number. Saying goodbye to her yesterday afternoon, he had given her the number and said, "Call me whenever you have to talk to someone about it."

A woman answered the telephone. There were party noises, buzz-buzz, laughter, a piano being played. "Yes, who is it?" She had a French-accented voice.

Johanna said who she was and, already regretting her call, asked, "Is Sam there?"

"Sammy!" the woman cried as though holding the receiver a little away from her. "Sam-*mee*, telephone for you!" The voice said very clearly that she belonged there and that she belonged to him.

There was a wait that felt long, perhaps a minute. The party noises rose and fell; there must be a great many people at his apartment. And she about to burst in with, "Sorry to interrupt you, but I thought I remembered hearing something peculiar last May when I . . ." She quietly hung up.

Her telephone rang a minute later. Sam said, "I don't know that many Johannas, it must have been you just now. My mother came looking for me and by the time I fought my way through the crowd—"

"Who?"

"My mother. She's staying here for a week or so."

Feeling embarrassment, relief, and obscure shame, she said blunderingly, "I didn't know you had all those people there. It's probably nothing, or nothing that won't keep until tomorrow. Thank you for calling back. Goodnight, Sam."

Idiot! she accused herself vehemently. *Ass.* Having her stomach drop away because there was someone there with him who had a perfect right to him. His *mother.* Well, that explained the Gallic shaping of his face. And it wasn't any of her business if he had half a dozen alluring-sounding French women in residence, none of whom was his mother.

Several minutes later the doorbell rang. For a fleeting second she thought, That's Sam, he always comes when—but he lived on Seventy-ninth Street, forty-two blocks away.

Alice Smith, seen through the eyehole, stood outside in the dim hall. Oh God. Johanna opened the door and tried to summon a polite face. Alice came in, put down on the floor a small overnight bag, and threw her arms around her.

"I had to be with you. I couldn't come yesterday because I had to work and it isn't something you call on the phone about. I cried all night."

Either, Johanna thought in what she realized was an unkindly fashion, you have a very soft heart, or a very soft head. A man you have never even laid eyes on.

Explanations followed rapidly. Alice had intended to arrive earlier in the evening but there had been a forty-minute delay while the train just sat in the station at Newark, and then she couldn't get a cab for ages, and—

Johanna, half listening, was thinking rapidly. What was she planning to do here, besides joining in, or instituting, a family mourning session for John Swain?

Answering her in a way, Alice Smith said in her sweet young iron voice, "I felt I couldn't possibly leave you alone. Waiting and watching and listening to see if they'd found him yet. I wanted us to be together." For the first time she seemed to become aware of Johanna's nightdress. "But you were in bed, did I wake you? Get right back in and I'll bring you something—hot milk or something."

She can't be, but she is, Johanna thought with horror, planning to stay here. Why? Not by nature anybody's victim, she said, "I'm sorry if you'd thought about staying the night but this as you see is a one-room apartment. Though it was very kind of you to come to offer comfort."

Alice glanced around the room. "I'm a tiny one. I can curl up on your love seat. I'm afraid it's too late to go wandering around in the night looking for a hotel room." What seemed to be genuine tears of hurt and grief filled her eyes. "After all, our own *father*." She put a hand to her mouth. "That just slipped out. Stanley saw it in the *Times* and told me."

Making no attempt, as none was possible, to explain her second-cousin lie, Johanna said, "Suppose we both have a drink. And then I'll get out linens. *For the night.*"

"Oh, thank you, I don't drink but I'll just make myself a nice cup of tea to keep you company. Don't bother yourself, I'll find out where things are."

Sitting looking gloomingly at an unwanted scotch and water, Johanna heard her bustling about in the kitchen, opening drawers and cabinets. What was there about Alice Smith that made her seem quite unreal? Was it that she was faking all this, wanting to be with her "family"? Was she really only here to monitor phone calls, spy on possible comings and goings, squirrel her way into a mythical group of Swains, take her place within the group, and perhaps eventually lay hands on the money any father's daughter would expect upon his death?

Coming back with a cup of tea, Alice seated herself in the slipper chair in the corner by the casement windows and said, "Will there be a memorial service? They do have those, don't they, when there isn't any . . . any body. I'd certainly want to be at the memorial service."

"I have no idea."

"But if there was one, wouldn't you be the person to arrange it? If you'd rather I did it . . . ? At least, when they're sure he's really—really gone. And there's another thing. Who's to take care of his things, see to them? They must be stored somewhere. Furniture, clothes, maybe a lot of his paintings." She took a dainty sip of her tea.

Now we are coming to the point, Johanna thought. Where are John Swain's worldly goods?

She heard the next question before it was spoken.

"Are you his heir?"

"You may or may not know my mother remarried when I was three, and I am to all intents and purposes a Landis, not a Swain." Her tone was quiet, cold, and formal.

"Yes, but that," Alice said patiently, "isn't really an answer. He could have—"

"Then to put it more clearly the answer is no."

The doorbell rang again. This time it was Sam Hines.

"I thought that—calling, you might want me for something or other." He gave her face an anxious and close examination and then his eye lit with barely concealed and profound disfavor on Alice sitting immovably, smiling over her teacup, in her chair. Johanna sensed that his arms had been ready to take her without delay or ceremony. Now they remained at his sides.

"This is a—" Johanna began. A what? A disaster in several ways. "A relative, Alice Smith. She's staying the night."

"In that case, will your guest excuse us a moment?" They were still in the hall, by the door across from the kitchen that led into a tiny dressing room and then to the bathroom. Sam opened the door and closed it firmly behind them. He looked at her in her hastily pulled-on robe and raised his eyebrows. "A chaperone?" he murmured, and Johanna, watching his expressive mouth, echoed its lifted corners: her first smile in two days.

"I'll explain her later, once I explain her to myself," she murmured back. "And as you were kind enough to leave your party for me, I'll tell you why I called you."

Glancing at the door, on the other side of which Alice might well be listening, she gestured him into the bathroom with her, closed that door too, and turned on the hot and cold water faucets in the sink. She repeated his Aunt Maggie's laughing prophetic statement.

He gave her a long stare punctuated by a blink. Then, instead of offering her a clarifying answer, or theory, or explanation ("Maggie's a nut, often her conversation makes no sense whatever") he asked her a question.

"What, uncensored—instinctive—was your own first gut reaction to this?"

"That for some reason he's chosen to disappear. That he isn't dead at all. Probably mad on my part, self-delusion. Snatching at straws."

"I'll have to circle around this for a bit." He looked past her, intent and frowning, looking into his Aunt Maggie's face, she suspected. "Obviously I can't, directly, quote her to her, or not yet. And for God's sake, Johanna, you never heard or overhead this statement. Promise me you'll bear that in mind?"

"Yes . . . why?"

"It might be, I know you'll think the word is crazy, dangerous."

Dangerous. The syllables seemed to shout over the sound of the rushing faucets. Now it was she who blinked. He put his hands on her shoulders and kissed her mouth lightly. "I can't think clearly in small Johanna'd spaces. I'll take myself off. And incidentally, please give Alice Smith a message for me. Tell her that, at this particular time, I wish she was in hell."

FIVE

Hurry, faster! said the engine of Matt Cummings' borrowed car as he drove northeast to Bride's Bay.

Get cracking, get in, get her back, before there's another man around to comfort her. After hearing with astonishment guiltily tinged with relief the news of John Swain's probable death, he had called her from New York and she had said in a clenched way, "I can't talk about it, not now. I don't want to see anyone, anyone at all. Goodbye, Matt."

He hadn't been able to start his headlong rush to her until this Saturday morning, a week after the disaster, because of his new job, if you could call it a job. Reporter and field man for the trade journal *Silver Annals*, under the masthead of which ran the words "Serving the Silverware World for the Past Seventy-five Years." It was the bottom of his professional barrel. He was merely filling in for a man on leave of absence for three months. His salary was eight thousand dollars a year. His editor was twenty-four, and when not dim on his drugs enjoyed putting this old-timer (an expression he used to Matt's face) through the hoops. "What have we got here, a rough draft?" as he looked through a finely honed article on the year's best-selling flatware patterns. "Sharpen it up, cut it by a third, give it a touch of the old pro. Under your byline it says, formerly with the New York *Times*. Remember?"

Don't think about him until Monday, push away the grind-

ing shame and rage, his nose rubbed daily in his own failure.
Think about Maggie, a world away from *Silver Annals*, and
now only about six hours away. He had started out at four
o'clock in the morning. With luck, he ought to be there between two and three. He might be able to sneak in an extra
day. Explain that he'd stopped off at the Reed & Barton silverware works in Taunton, Massachusetts, because he had an
idea for a piece on new developments in electroplating. He
might not, one way or another, need the job for long. At this
hopeful thought, his mouth twisted at one side into its stale,
bitter smile. Anyway, good luck or bad, he had to see her.

He had deliberately given her no warning of his visit. She
might flee. Taken by surprise, completely by surprise, she'd
have to open the door and let him in. Back into her life. After
reaching Bride's Bay, he circled the town instead of going
directly through it. When he reached the mailbox on Foxcoffin Road he turned into the drive and halfway up it pulled the
car off to one side behind a thick stand of balsam. Furtive?
Like hell. Just tactics.

Hands in his pockets, he walked the rest of the drive. At the
top, where the meadow opened out, he moved very swiftly to
the sheltering bulk of the barn. Swain's old car was parked
outside the garage. Maggie hadn't a car of her own. She must,
thank Christ, be home.

The deep grass around the house was roiled with tire tracks
and heavily trampled. Television trucks, newspaper people,
swarming to the colorful tragedy. All gone, now. Maggie left,
in silence, to her grief. Maggie, without Swain.

After the rainy week, the day was soft and sunny. The
breeze on his forehead informed him that his face was wet
with sweat. Nothing to be nervous about, afraid of. Just Maggie. Would she be downstairs, packing up Swain's things? No,
if she was, she'd have the doors open, on a day like this. The
back door was closed. He turned the corner of the house and
started, very quietly, up the outside stairway.

From above, the sound coming softly and merrily through
the screen door, he heard her singing. "In Dublin's fair city
where girls are so pretty . . ."

Perhaps there is nothing that suggests more vividly to the

ear peace, contentment—happiness—than the sound of a woman, alone, singing.

Singing? Matt was motionless on the stairs, halfway up. Was she drunk? No, the words were shaped with delicate clarity. "She wheeled her wheelbarrow through streets broad and narrow . . ." He had forgotten what a lovely voice she had.

Had she gone a little queer, from shock? Temporarily round the bend? No. There was no hysteria underlying the sweet casual fluting.

". . . crying cockles, and mussels, alive, alive-o." Water was abruptly turned on. She must be at the kitchen sink. After several minutes, it was turned off. There was a thump at what sounded like counter level. Washing something, dishes or clothes. If it was clothes, she would any minute now emerge to hang them on the line that went from the garage to a hook on the stairway rail.

To test possible hallucination against reality—after all, the exhausting twelve-hour drive had left him feeling like a zombie—he pressed himself against the clapboards of the house wall and listened hard to any other sounds that might be offered to him. The deep in-and-out breathing of the Atlantic on the shore at mid-tide. A light plane overhead. (Surely not, after a week, still looking for Swain?) The idle chirp of a yellow warbler in an old gnarled lilac near the foot of the steps.

His mind was going around in stunned frantic circles.

Had she, then, not been in love with Swain? But in some kind of thrall to him, and happy to be released from it?

No. He had furiously sensed between them the bond, the crackle.

Mentally and emotionally he was without a compass, lost. It was impossible.

It was real, true, still lying somewhere on the air, Maggie's carefree song.

All that he retained was caution. For some reason it seemed vitally important that she not know about his having heard her. He retreated down the stairs and around the house corner again. The old, thick lilac near the corner would allow in safety an occasional peek from behind it.

The screen door banged and he heard her footsteps on the stairs. She went, her back to him, to the clothesline and hung out a decorative wash, her own clothing and two sheets, brown-and-white-striped. She sauntered back, sat down on the bottom step of the stairway, reached into the pocket of her denim jacket, and took out a pear. Face lifted a little to the sunlight, she ate the pear with open pleasure, brushing away with her fingertips the trickle of juice down her chin. She is not only all right, surviving, he thought. She is happily and wholly herself.

After she went back up the stairs he waited five minutes, or what without his watch seemed to be five minutes. Then he walked into the center of the trampled grassy space and shouted, "Hey, Maggie! Look who's here!"

If he hadn't been still so badly jarred he might have been amused at the alteration in the woman who opened the screen door to him as he was running up the steps. All the light gone out of her face. Her hair disordered as if she didn't give a damn about anything. She must just have untidied it, deliberately.

He gave her a quick hug and then let her go. She said, her voice dulled and flat, "I suppose this is sweet of you, Matt, but I wish you hadn't."

"I would have been here sooner but I'm at last working." He told her about his job, making it sound better than it was, talking fast to fill the unwelcoming silence on her part.

"Well . . . good." Sounding as if it was an effort to form ordinary little words. Sounding as if she were far away, and alone with death.

On her hospitably open kitchen shelves along one wall, he saw an inviting collection of bottles. In a takeover manner (this poor woman incapable of lifting a finger) he made them both gin and tonics. He took her hand and led her into the living room. "Sit down, darling."

Maggie had been prepared for this incursion and was only surprised that it hadn't happened sooner.

"Now." He sat down beside her and leaned close. "What are your plans? Surely you're not going to stay here, all alone with—with your ghosts."

"No. I might go to Peggy Cleves in Boston or . . . I don't

know where." Remain fallen apart. It was simple once you got the hang of it. "Or Sam's, although . . . but there are things to be seen to, bills to be paid, his—" Stop and draw a breath on the word "his." "Clothes and things to be disposed of. This is only a rented house, you know, already that beastly man who owns it is clamoring—he wants it free and clear to rent as of the first of . . . what *is* next month?" Head bent, fingertips nervously touching her chignon.

"October. Isn't there anyone else to do this? Family or something?" He realized how little he knew about Swain's private life. "Who's his heir? Whoever it is might as well work for their money."

Maggie had no idea whether in some press account of the drowning she might have been named as his heir; or would be in the near future. Thank God for that girl's brief visit, back in May.

"I am. But it may be entirely academic. He warned me there would probably someday be a court fight over it, there was a daughter who was shaking her fist and making ridiculous demands, financial ones, even before he . . . It might be years before I ever saw a penny, if then." Careful. Don't sound greedy and practical about Swain's will. "Not that it matters. I must, I absolutely must, Matt, take one of my tranquilizers and nap for a while . . . or at least go away into some kind of . . ."

"Of course, darling. I could use a nap here on the couch myself after that drive and then later I'll make supper for us. I have only the weekend but at least I can see you get some rest and something to eat. Tomorrow if you want I'll finish up with all the rest of that grisly business downstairs."

But he didn't take a nap. He couldn't sit still. He began roaming the room.

His intuitions had not yet sent their conclusion to his brain.

He found himself opening the slant-front desk and peering at the untidiness within. Maggie said that life was too short for arranging pieces of paper. What was he doing? What was he looking for? If anything?

It couldn't be possible. But it mysteriously hinted at itself like the distant flickering suggestion of flame under the sensuous billows of Swain's paintings.

Who would have the gall?
Swain would have the gall.
Maggie would have the gall.
Adrian de Lima would have the gall.

He felt like a dowser with his forked hazel switch in hand,
seeking a location for a well in a land where water couldn't
exist. But there it was, the downward twitch of the infallible
hazel. Water there, below. Deep, dark water.

Gall. A good word to seize on. A good theme to work with.
Now what could he . . . ? Matt Cummings would have the gall
too. But the gall for, in his case, what?

He was still staring at the litter in the desk: bills, letters, a
box of buttons, her passport. Was he in some foreign land,
Swain? And not that dark bourn of Hamlet's from which no
traveler returns. He picked up her green leather address book.
She wouldn't write such a thing down, name, address, telephone number, would she? He found a pencil in one of the
cubbyholes and on the back of the envelope of her telephone
bill copied out the last ten entries. No names, just initials,
some of them with only phone numbers, two of them S'n. He
kept glancing nervously over his shoulder but there was no
sound from the bedroom. Of course not. She was prostrated,
wasn't she?

To return to practical matters, she was the last person in the
world to wonder what had happened to the envelope her
telephone bill was in. He turned it over and looked at the date:
mailed the day before yesterday. Inspiration struck. He
removed the slip of paper listing message charges, number
called, place called, time spent on the call. Maggie made ex-
travagant use of the Bell System and thought nothing of a
twenty-minute chat with a friend in Seattle. She wouldn't
wonder what had happened to that either. He put the envelope
and the message slip into his wallet and was surprised to find
that his hands were shaking. He closed the desk flap.

Go back over it once again.

The drowning, or disappearance, or however you liked to
put it, taking place only a few weeks before Swain's big-smash
show in New York.

Maggie, thinking herself unseen and unheard, happy and
whole. Singing to herself as she did her washing. Eating a pear

in the sun. Then, when her visitor officially arrived, being just what she would be expected to be—shot to hell.

The choice of the song was surely a coincidence; it had always been one of her favorite ballads. But—

"Alive, alive-o."

He didn't after all sneak in an extra day. He left after lunch on Sunday, having tenderly served Maggie sautéed mushrooms on toast of which she managed only a bite. She wouldn't hear of his helping out downstairs, going through Swain's things, the funereal clear-up. "No, no, I must do it myself. Only I will know what I want to keep, of his."

Well, naturally she wouldn't hear of it. Swain might have left some forgotten clue, hint, careless scribble.

By now the impossible had become in Matt's mind the perfectly, daringly possible.

"Bye, darling. I'll be in touch. I'd certainly head for Sam's if I were you. New York's your own stamping ground, you know. And could you, of all people, miss the retrospective?"

S I X

One of Matt's duties at *Silver Annals* was to open the mail. On Friday he had come upon a lengthy public relations puff from Renwick Silversmiths in Peekskill, New York, announcing their new line of silver jewelry for men and women, authentically copied from world-famous museum pieces. He called in Monday morning and told the yawning Linda, who lived with the editor and owner and felt that that, on the whole, constituted enough work for her salary, "I heard about something hot in Peekskill. Renwick. Very hush-hush. I'm going to take a run up there today and see what I can find out."

All he'd have to do was rearrange and retype the publicity release, which would take him about ten minutes, and would wait until this evening. He was now living in a rooming house far west on Fourteenth Street between Eighth Avenue and Ninth. The telephone in the front hall wouldn't do at all for his purpose. Too wearisome, getting barrels of change. And people coming and going, and wanting to use the phone themselves, or waiting somewhat hopelessly for rooming-house messages which he would be preventing from being received.

Fortunately he had not, on quitting Joe Rainey's, returned the extra key to his apartment. Joe would be at work by now, but just for safety's sake he called him on the hall phone. No answer. Good. When Rainey's telephone bill came in, how could he know who had run up all those frightful charges?

Unless he, Matt, struck oil with the first few calls.

Might as well walk, try to start to get back into some kind of shape for the task ahead, whatever it was. The distance was a brisk twenty-seven blocks. For the first time in years there was a purpose and power in his stride.

To deal with the short list—the message slip from the telephone bill—he took the precaution of stopping at a public telephone booth a block before Joe's. There were eighteen long-distance calls listed but only the ones following Friday, September 14, were of any use to him. Conceivably, in her panic, her grief, she might have been expected to call everybody she knew. But there were only three calls after the fatal date. Two to Seashell Park, New Jersey, one on the sixteenth, the second on the seventeenth, each call lasting close to thirty minutes. The New York call, on the seventeenth, had taken up eleven minutes. His instinct going clickety-click, he looked up the de Lima Gallery in the directory. Same number for the New York call.

Seashell Park didn't sound at all like a Maggie kind of place. Cape May, or Stone Harbor, yes; places where attractive people might be found. It was the obscure sound of this Jersey town which had dictated his choice of the phone booth. The other calls he would have to make, from the entries in her address book, seemed comfortably remote and anonymously selected: Seattle, El Paso, Paris, Chicago, Los Angeles, New York, London.

He didn't want Seashell Park turning up on Joe Rainey's message slip. It was the sort of place name which might lodge in somebody else's head too.

He stood thinking a moment before dropping in his coin. He was reasonably sure there would be no one in residence with Swain—if indeed this wasn't a wild-goose call. The more people allowed into any plot, the greater the danger. Keep it tight, small, and safe.

Tune up your ear, chum, he advised himself. Even if the voice answering the phone was disguised, or handkerchief-muffled, he thought he would recognize it.

Ninety-nine chances out of a hundred, Seashell Park wouldn't produce a damned thing. Eight chances out of ten, there would be nobody at home when the telephone rang.

But go ahead. Don't just stand here, sweating.

The operator when given the number told him to deposit one dollar and fifty cents in coins, please. One ring. Two. Three.

"Hello?" said John Swain's voice.

But make him say another word or two, just to be absolutely, *absolutely*—

The pounding of his heart could be affecting his hearing.

"Who is this?" demanded Swain. "What number did you want?"

Matt hung up. He was momentarily caught in a grayed haze. He put out a hand to the wall of the booth to support himself. Then, leaving the booth, he continued up the block to Joe's apartment building. It was only when he was opening the glass door to the lobby that he realized that now he had no earthly reason for this unauthorized visit.

Swain and de Lima had discussed the matter of the telephone. "We could get you switched over to an unlisted number," de Lima said. "But if your landlady wanted for some reason to get in touch with her tenant she might just wonder why a pleasant colorless retired insurance man requires an unlisted number. And your neighbors, if any, might wonder too, when wishing to call you up to invite you to a nice hand of pinochle, or an evening of bowling. It's only a little boat. Let us not rock it."

His number, or rather the number listed for Coe, Helena L., in the Ocean County directory, must resemble in its digital makeup someone else's number. Twice he had gotten wrong-number calls, one from a man, one from a small boy, asking, "Is Artie there?"

No doubt this call, just aborted, was from someone wanting Artie too. Silences, breathing silences, on the other end of the line are always unnerving but there are people not very fast on their mental feet who think things over, decide that this couldn't be the right voice answering the telephone; and without so much as a "sorry" hang up. There were even those who, not getting the number they wanted, felt that some kind of mysterious dirty trick had been played on them.

To hell with Artie. Swain went back to his morning stint: a

chapter of the thick paperback *Insurance in All Its Aspects: A Working Compendium for Professionals and Laymen.* "Study it well, John," said de Lima.

Matt, whose memory was still retentive, called the law firm of Landis and Landis to request the number at which Johanna Landis could be contacted during the day. Three tries at half-hour intervals of her home phone number had announced her as being elsewhere.

Reaching her at UBC, he adopted a slight Maine twang. "This is Walt Williams of the Tinkertown, Maine, *Gazette*, Miss Landis. First off, sorry for your terrible loss. Now then, is it true that you are planning to take your father's designated heir, Margaret Lind, to law? A court fight? Word around here's that a lot of money is going to be at stake. From his paintings."

Her startled indignation was entirely convincing. "Absolutely not!"

"By that you mean, not right now?"

"By that I mean, never. Goodbye, Mr. Williams."

His next stop was at a Gulf station on West Fifteenth Street. He asked for and obtained a map of New Jersey and retired to his room to study it. Seashell Park turned out to be in Ocean County. Out again, to a public phone booth. He wasn't yet at all sure why, but he didn't want any fellow roomer to hear him enunciating Ocean County, or Seashell Park.

He called Ocean County information, gave the Seashell Park number, and asked to know under what name it was listed, Helena Coe. Without much hope of success, he wheedled, "And the address, there's a good girl?" Sorry, addresses not given out.

Helena Coe. Another conspirator? Or, in a coast town, maybe a sublet? Lonely empty houses by the cold sea. Mmmmm.

He would have to go down there and reconnoiter. Lay hands on the Ocean County directory, look up Helena Coe's address. And find out, silently and unseen, if the man living in the house was John Swain.

Because already he was beginning to doubt his ears. He had so badly wanted it to be the voice that perhaps he had brainwashed himself into thinking he recognized it. Stop and listen in memory to Swain's voice. No accent, which of course was in itself a kind of accent. Educated. Resonant. No nasal overtones. There must be a thousand, a hundred thousand, such voices in New York, New Jersey, Connecticut, Pennsylvania, before you began at all compass points to hit geographically identifying styles of speech.

Until the thing was a certainty, there was no point in cluttering his mind with plans and possibilities. Find out, and then see what was to be done about it. Done with it. He found himself thinking of the title of a short story by F. Scott Fitzgerald, "The Diamond as Big as the Ritz."

He was back in his room now and in the mirror over the dresser caught his reflection grinning. Horrible rictus grin in the flawed mirror, crazy desperate nut kind of man in a shabby room, bloodshot blue eyes bulging out of his head, grinning all by himself. Watch it, Mac, he said sharply to himself. Was all this a mirage in his personal desert?

Have to wait until the weekend to investigate. His hunt must be undertaken after dark; Matt Cummings must not be opened from some window hunting John Swain in Seashell Park. And if and when he did locate the right house, what if the lights were out and the occupant of the house asleep? He could hardly knock on the door and wake the man to examine his features in convenient close-up.

Anyway, this was not the time to do something, anything, about Swain—when he was feeling ill and confused, hot and cold, on a brink he didn't quite comprehend.

And if the ghost was there, he was *there*, living there. He obviously hadn't just dropped by to answer the telephone. He would keep. Until time allowed a rational, thought-out program of operation, not a half-assed dash to Jersey right away. He couldn't dare steal an extra day tomorrow for the Renwick story in Peekskill; it could very possibly cost him his job. He had run out of cars to borrow; and he needed, he reminded himself grimly, even the small change *Silver Annals* paid him, to finance what would have to be a trip by bus, or buses, to Ocean County.

SEVEN

"You can't mean to tell me, Adrian, that everything's gone?" cried Lily Patchester.

"With a possible exception," de Lima said, raising his voice as he had to be heard above the successful din of John Swain's retrospective. "I have in hand your offer by cable for 'Number Seventy-one.' But it's been topped by thirty thousand dollars."

"By whom?" Lily asked with possessive suspicion. She considered John Swain more or less her own property; it was she who had been his first spectacular patron.

De Lima, straight-faced, named the chemical fertilizer heiress Lily considered her foremost rival in appearance, money, and collecting bravura.

"You could be lying through your teeth, but all right, I'll meet it."

"Meet it, Lily? Top it."

"You look so rich and happy tonight one forgets you're a businessman, Adrian. Done, then—at two hundred thousand and *one* dollars."

She blinked slightly at a nearby flash from a *Women's Wear Daily* camera. The cameras of *Vogue* and the New York *Times* were on hand too. In de Lima's judiciously edited lexicon, everybody in New York was there tonight, along with globally selected guests. The first night of the show was by invitation only but of course there were party crashers; if there weren't, one should enclose oneself in one's professional casket.

Just inside the gallery door was a five-by-five-foot black-and-white photograph of the Star boat lashed in foam, displaying against the harsh rocks its broken mast. People entering passed it in proper subdued silence and then six feet farther on resumed their celebrating chatter and laughter and shrieks of greeting to friends.

"A vulgar touch, that photograph," said the dealer Perry Giovanniantonio, an uninvited guest, to the dealer Mark Ryder, also uninvited.

"You should be so vulgar," said Ryder.

Both of them were busily eating caviar at one of three splendid buffets. Approaching them, de Lima said jovially, "Go ahead, gentleman, feast on tragedy."

"Just picking up crumbs from your table, as it were," Giovanniantonio said. "You're sold out, I hear on every side, even this early in the game. I suppose you have a few more Swains clutched to your breast against the time when the prices instead of doubling start to quadruple?"

"To put a new use to an old phrase," de Lima said blandly, "precious few."

Ryder helped himself to a glass of champagne from a tray being carried past him. He drank deeply and then lifted his glass to de Lima. "To put an altered spelling to an old phrase," inclining his head toward the photograph at the entrance, "a *fate* accompli."

"What hornets we brethren are, aren't we," de Lima murmured, turning away to fling his arms around a tall thin woman in a four thousand-dollar bugle-beaded tank-top Halston. "Rosie darling!"

"It must be nice to pocket well in excess of a million dollars on a wet Friday night between eight and nine-fifteen," said the Halstoned woman. "Or at least that's what they're saying."

"Indeed I wish it were my pocket," de Lima sighed.

"Nonsense, your cut is thirty percent as I remember. I'm told Maggie's his heir. I see she managed to choke back her tears and make it to your party."

"She could hardly not have come to what would have been in many ways the most important night of Swain's life. In a sense this is his memorial service."

"A very jolly one, I must say. One scarcely finds such buckets of Beluga anywhere, anymore."

Maggie, looking as quiet and understated as it was possible for a woman of her appearance to look, wore black, long and slender and, no matter what her intentions, seductive. There was an aloneness about her, partly projected from within and partly provided by the partygoers, most of whom did not want to approach her and talk about anything as dreary as death. Not with de Lima's magnificent wells to drink at, and his buffets to nibble at. And everyone they knew to amuse themselves with; or about, when he or she had moved away to another knot of talk and laughter.

"Got you!" said a triumphant voice behind her. Maggie spun around to Sam Hines, another uninvited guest.

Her sudden motion spilled champagne from her glass to her shoulder. "You scared me!"

He gave her a one-armed hug and a kiss on the cheek. "As there seemed no other way to see my aunt, I thought you'd be here if you were anywhere."

He had been trying since Sunday to get in touch with her. There had been no answer to a number of calls to Bride's Bay and he thought she had probably done the sensible thing and left. He called several of her friends in New York and several more called him to ask him if he had any idea where Maggie was.

Replying to his unspoken question, she said, "I've been staying by myself at a hotel. I couldn't face the kind tides of sympathy."

Sam, a man of two countries, fell easily into French ambiguities.

"It must be hard for you up there on your tightrope."

"What tightrope?"

She had a way of flaring her eyes when she was startled. They flared now.

Watching her closely, he said, "Oh well . . . to grieve and yet . . . all this blaze of glory, belated as it is, coming to Swain . . . you can't help but feel . . ."

She didn't have a giveaway face; the shape of her bones kept it composed. But knowing her well he felt an emanation of some sort of leaping inner turmoil. Which could mean something or nothing—nothing in that it was merely the stimulus of this brilliant night in John Swain's honor.

She put what seemed to him a nervous hand to her cheek to protect herself from his intent eyes. And then looking past him cried with what he thought was immense relief, "Matt darling! How sweet of you."

Matt, among all these handsome people, looked shabby and odd enough, in his defiantly strutting short-legged way, to be judged by them as some sort of personage, such as a critic or an eccentric, obscure millionaire. He moved past Sam to put his arms around her. "Maggie *dear*," he said. "I thought I could be of some help. At least see you home and tuck you in when this ordeal is ended. Hello, Sam. I'll take over now."

"What hotel are you at, Maggie?" Sam asked. After a slight hesitation, she said, "The Barclay."

"Come and stay with me. I'd feel better having you under my eye. And I won't offer you more sympathy than you can put up with." She might or might not be able or willing to read between his lines.

I don't care what you're up to, what Swain may be up to, you're safe with me.

All he really wanted to do was to get Johanna Swain Landis off the hook of loss and sadness. Beyond that he had no intention of pursuing investigations. Let Swain play dead if he wished, let the waterfalls of money pour into a numbered account in Switzerland—if that was what this death was all about. In methods of turning a dollar, everyone to his own taste.

"Thank you, darling. I'll think it over. And now, my hungry Matt, come with me and we'll catch you up on all the caviar you haven't eaten in years. Goodnight, Sam. In case either of us gets lost in the crush."

Deciding he had learned as much in a few minutes as he would in the entire evening, now that she was on her guard (and deciding at the same time to believe for the moment in the wisdom of the bones over and above the brain) Sam was about to leave when he saw, in a far corner, Alice Smith.

• • •

"You wouldn't have the nerve," Stan Parker said. "First-night kind of thing, dress-up, champagne, the works, probably by invitation only."

"Who has a better right to be there?" Alice asked calmly.

But she gave her entry a little thought. If it started at eight, there ought to be people swarming around by nine. Easier to get in, perhaps join herself to a group just getting out of a taxi. On the train from Trenton, her gossamer short dress of pale blue lace over chiffon was covered up by a rose-colored rain cape. She carried her overnight bag and an umbrella. Thank heavens wet weather did nice and not awful things to her hair, made it spring into tender tiny petals around her forehead. It was caught back with a blue velvet ribbon.

In the ladies' room at Penn Station, she redid her face and thought how very young she looked, and how, well, pretty. There was a wait for a cab on the ramp but it wouldn't hurt to be even a little later.

Lucy Delft was doing her stint of duty at the door. She had her invitation list in hand. "Good evening. Your name is—?"

"Smith, Alice Smith. I didn't get an invitation because I suppose a lot of people don't know."

"Don't know what?"

"That I'm John Swain's daughter."

Rather than cause an unseemly commotion at the entrance with whom Lucy Delft instantly considered this little bitch, she let her pass, got someone else to take over at the door, and went immediately in search of de Lima.

"Probably nothing, Adrian, but there's a creature here who claims to be Swain's daughter."

De Lima, sharply on the alert, said, "Is her name Johanna?"

"No. Alice Smith."

This sounded to him ominously like a pseudonym. Johanna Landis, come to calculate her father's worth as it would be seen in hard cash tonight. Already laying devious plans to get her hands on some of it. It had been too much to hope that she would keep her distance.

"She's over there, in that sweet little Alice blue gown."

De Lima was torn. He would have preferred to ignore her

existence. But he felt he must know her intentions, if any, to arm himself.

Alice was standing dazzled, looking at all the people, rich people, collected here for her own *father*. And the paintings, walls and walls of them, towering to the ceilings, in a dizzying soft sea of color. She had had her hopes but she hadn't expected anything like this. Like a movie, but it was real.

She held a glass in her hand. A nice middle-aged man with a foreign accent had said, "May I get you something, my dear? Champagne?"

"I don't drink." Controlled dainty voice.

"Very sensible. I suppose that's why you look so pristine. Then some Perrier water." He brought her this and went off to refresh his watery scotch. "Save a place at your side and at your service for me."

She looked and sounded harmless enough but de Lima felt he might be dealing with an unexploded bomb. What if she were mad as a hatter, and suddenly started screaming about lawsuits, in front of people who had just invested heavily in John Swain.

He went over to her and murmured in her ear, "Your presence is an honor indeed. I am Adrian de Lima. Suppose we seek for a moment the privacy of my office."

Alice, who thought she was going to be scolded, and then arrested for trespass, or at the least thrown out, said, "I haven't done anything wrong. He's my father, John Swain is."

Two people a foot away were listening with vivid interest. De Lima took her hand. "No, no—a comfortable chat. Old times, family, and so on." His smile was benevolent. "Special people deserve special attention."

Alice found herself in what must be his office but looked like a living room in a home-decorating magazine. He seated her on the love seat. "Now then, what is your name again? Johanna?"

"No. She said she was his cousin once removed but she was lying, she's actually his daughter. I don't know what she's up to."

De Lima, oriental in his own mental processes, was inwardly very much alarmed. Johanna Landis under the false name Alice Smith accusing herself of being a liar. What could possibly be behind it all?

Alice, who didn't care for the word illegitimate, said, "I'm his what they call natural daughter." For further clarification, she added, "A love child." She looked up at him with her innocent blue eyes.

Good God, this was frightful—if true. And how many more love children might Swain have scattered about the landscape?

Not knowing for a moment what to say, what dangerous bog he might sink a foot into, de Lima maintained a watchful silence. The horrid thought struck him that there might be considered to be a likeness about the shape of the eyebrows and the turn of the forehead bone. But don't look for danger where none, it was to be hoped, existed. Probably she was here only to share in her putative father's triumph.

New Jersey, his infallible instinct for placing people, docketing them, told him. Working girl, secretary or some such thing. Family of no great account.

Alice had rehearsed her question on the train. Be forthright. Be businesslike. Don't let people get away with anything. Right is right. "Who," she asked, "is his trustee, or maybe there are more than one? I thought you might know."

De Lima pursed his lips and unpursed them. "I am his sole trustee."

"Then—not tonight, of course, he's not here—my lawyer will be making an appointment with you."

He walked away to lean on his music stand, facing her, in a position of authority.

"This is probably entirely academic, but you are aware of something generally called the statute of limitations? In the state of Maine, it is five years."

"Yes, my lawyer told me, but"—Alice smiled seraphically —"I'm young."

"Odd that your father never mentioned you."

"I think he didn't know about me. It would have been sort of awkward, my mother with her two children later by my sort-of-father. He adopted me. But Mr. Swain, my father, *might* have known and put something by for me he wanted me to have. That's why I want to go through his things."

"What things?" De Lima, who seldom smoked, helped

himself to a cigarette from an ebony box.

"There must be clothes and furniture to go through and take care of. And who knows? piles of paintings. I mean, if he died that suddenly, you wouldn't necessarily know about them either, would you? And I heard a woman out there telling a man the painting they were standing under sold for a hundred and seventy-five thousand dollars."

The only way to dispose of this young leech for the time being was to appear to accommodate her.

Sounding casual, unconcerned, he said, "If and when your bona fides are established, you might be able to get in touch with the heir, who was also Swain's tenant. She would know where his effects are stored and—"

The office door was opened abruptly. Lucy Delft said, "Adrian, *quick*. Lily and Mrs. Frey are having a terrible fight about who owns 'Number Seventy-one.' " In verification of this, a scream was heard from the more distant of the two galleries.

De Lima swept off and Alice sat and waited on the love seat. The desire struck her to seek a bathroom. The excitement, maybe, and she'd stayed nice and cool if she had to say so herself. Perhaps there's a private one opening from the office. like in Mr. Berlin's office at the store.

There was. She was a little awed by the size, the lilac-beige marble, the recessed tub, and the shower stall hung in heavy purple linen. Like an emperor, she thought. But where was the—? Oh. In another little separate room to the right of the shower, and it looked funny. A bidet? She'd heard of bidets but never seen one.

Washing her hands, she admired the immense oval sink. If there was going to be money, real money, sometime in the not-too-distant future, it would be nice getting used to it. Living like this.

Not liking to be seen emerging from a bathroom—it was somehow not quite nice in front of a strange man—she opened the door a crack to see if de Lima had come back to the office. She saw the opposite door open and a tall woman in black came in, closing the door quietly behind her. She went swiftly to the telephone. Alice narrowed her crack, but she could still hear.

"Darling! I promised and here I am but I mustn't allow more than a split second. Beyond your wildest dreams, and mine. Everything's gone, I'll give you the figures when I see you. Right now two women are having a bloody battle over you, Lily Patchester's one of them. See your morning *Times*. Now I must hang up."

There was the click of the receiver being replaced and the woman in black left the office. As she opened the far door Alice heard another distant scream. Get out, get out, fast, before he came back. She circled three animated groups and stopped to get back some breath while she gazed at a painting she didn't see.

A man's voice said, "Alice Smith, isn't it?"

She turned, obscurely terrified, to see the man Johanna Landis had said was Sam Hines, last Sunday night after he'd left Johanna's apartment. Rude man, who'd snatched her away to talk to her alone in the little dressing room.

He in turn had been filled in by Johanna on Alice's family claims. His first brief irritated impression of her was fortified; there was no need to ask her what, with her daintily grabbing fingers, she was doing here, although she wasn't the kind of person who would turn up on a de Lima invitation list.

Her mind a ringing void, she said, just to have words in her mouth, "Johanna isn't here—or I haven't seen her—but I thought I might be able to stay at her apartment tonight . . ."

"She's out of town but then she almost always is," Sam lied at speed.

He hadn't remembered that the blue eyes had such an odd, rounded blankness to them.

As though she hadn't been listening, ". . . except that I've changed my mind. I'm all . . . well, you know, the excitement. I think I'll go straight back home."

De Lima, lightly patting his forehead with his handkerchief, said, "Evening Sam. Where's that girl I saw you talking to just now?"

"She left."

"Ah." De Lima put his handkerchief away. "Thank—at least for the moment—God."

EIGHT

Mrs. Paglieri, who ran the Dory Dune, was pleased to get a little out-of-season business even if it was only for a night or two. And the man looked respectable enough, and carried what could be loosely called luggage, an old black leather duffle bag.

Signing her register, Matt wrote "Joseph Matthews." He was conducted to a room furnished in blindingly shellacked maple and daffodil-print cotton on the bed, at the windows, and skirting the dressing table. In spite of its determined attempt at cheer it smelled of damp and mold, and as he opened the closet to hang up his raincoat he heard something scuttling away.

He looked at his watch. Eight-twenty. He had started from New York in mid-afternoon. What if you had to live your whole life with buses as your sole transportation, made to wait between connections like all those faceless people?

What reason did he have to think he wouldn't live his whole life, or whatever remained of it, with buses?

Speaking of faceless—He tried on the hat he had bought at Macy's in the morning. He had never in his life worn a hat and he thought it might offer some sort of protective anti-identification. He had crushed it in his fists and stepped on it to try to take away some of the aggressive newness of the hat. But at night, in the dark, a hat was a hat.

He allowed himself one sparing tot from the bottle in his duffle bag and then went down to the room Mrs. Paglieri had pointed out as the Sea Lounge. "Feel free, Mr. Matthews," she had said. With its blood-colored vinyl chairs and sofa and its piles of curly old magazines it reminded him of an unfashionable dentist's waiting room. There was a coin telephone on the wall, the Ocean County directory hanging under it.

Coe, Helena L., 667 Parade Street. Unwise to ask Mrs. Paglieri where Parade Street was from here. Go find it. The town wasn't that large.

No need to feel so nerved up. This was a voyage purely of investigation. Call it a ghost-laying. No action or actions planned. Not now, not yet. Raincoated and hatted, he went out into the damp dark. The rain had stopped but the air was heavy. Was that why he found it a little hard to breathe?

There were no mysterious lanes or winding ways to trudge. Seashell Park was laid out in a flat grid pattern. The streetlights were few and far between. Many of the houses were dark. He was wearily prepared for blocks and blocks, back and forth, up and down, quartering the town.

Parade Street was the next street over.

One block nearer the sea than his own street, Ocean Boulevard. Feeling the imaginary gaze of invisible eyes behind darkened windows studying him, Matt hunched into himself, and when he had to pass under a streetlight walked faster.

Number 667, here you are. A small spare house, projecting screened porch in front, barely sketching itself in the distant mercury-blue light from the end of the block. Windows, all of them, dark.

The house next door was only about twenty feet from 667. Someone there, but shades pulled to the sills of two lighted windows on the lower floor. Occupants invisible, but then so was he unless someone came out for a breath of air.

He felt something against his ankle and almost cried out aloud. Christ. A cat. Was it Swain's cat? You madman, Swain is fathoms deep in the Atlantic. The fish will have gotten at him. But then, whom had Maggie been calling? When the phone rang in this silent darkened house, who had answered it?

Maybe Swain had taken fright at Matt's own mute telephone call. Packed his bags, gone to another anonymous town.

Rusted-over reporter's instincts made him go up the cement drive and past the open, empty side garage to the rear of the house. Sand underfoot, stairway to a little deck outside a door. Was this the bedroom, at the back? Would he be asleep at his hour?

Hardly. If there was a watering hole open in this desolate place, he might be drowning a drink or two. How would I be feeling now, Matt asked himself, if I were Swain and I were alive? I'd have read the coverage of the opening in the *Times*. And might have had a phone call from de Lima. I would be bursting with joy and triumph—and find myself going a little nutty because of having no one to share it with.

His ear picked up a sound at the front. The screen door of the porch closing, not banging. He went to the stairs, a two-sided flight, and hid himself in the space under them. Lights went on, shades were snapped down. Private kind of fellow who had just arrived here. Or woman, there was no way of telling yet. Perhaps—logically, and the bottom dropping out of everything—the owner, Helena Coe.

The telephone, ringing, sounded frighteningly near. Looking up through the wooden slats of the deck, Matt noticed that the window above was open three inches or so at the bottom. "Hello?" said the voice that sounded so like Swain's. "Oh. Thank you very much, but I'm no good at Scrabble. And I've got to type up my notes from today—shells on the beach. I'll be working late." After a few seconds of silence, an alarmed, "Oh, please don't bother. I never eat sweets, my indigestion is—" The other party must have terminated the call.

"Hell and damnation," said the voice which didn't just sound like Swain's. Was Swain's. A door closed, what must be a door on the near side in the next house over. A flashlight pierced the darkness of the backyard. Matt huddled under his stairs, pressed against the house wall. Feet went up the stairs and paused over his head. Light knock, door opening. "My brownies never gave anyone indigestion," said the woman. "And I've brought you the evening paper, I didn't know if you had one. I think this fresh air must be doing you good, you look stronger already."

"Well, thank you—very kind."

"If not Scrabble, a quick hand of gin and," laughing, "a snort of Bourbon?"

"No, no. I really must work."

"All right, goodnight, I'll pry you loose yet, see if I don't. I'm still working on who you remind me of. Why do I connect you with Morristown? Or was that someone else? 'Night again."

If she shone her flashlight vertically, would she see him through the slats? The spaces between were about a quarter of an inch wide. She angled the light slantingly down the stairs. He heard her heavy sigh after the door closed, the defeat in the footsteps on the wooden treads.

Through the window, sounds of a man making himself a drink, ice cubes being pried from their tray, thump of a bottle set down. No point in staying here in his fetal position, curled against the house, because he had done what he had come here to do. He had found out.

"I've been hiding in your bedroom," said Maggie. "I let myself in as quietly as a foreign agent and I heard you talking to some woman out here. Darling."

Little clink as the drink was set down. Matt closed his eyes hard but he could see it, feel it, the embracing bodies. He knew exactly how every inch of her felt.

"Let's get out of this kitchen before she decides to bring me some homemade vegetable soup. Make yourself a drink while I . . ."

Window pulled down, sound of a locking device being turned in the back door. Light out. A float of her laughter, faint. Next stop, of course, the bedroom.

Matt rolled to his knees and got stiffly up. He found himself surprised at himself. Coronary kind of situation there, under the stairs, his heart should still be crashing with it. There should have been a second-to-second awful fear of discovery and with discovery disaster of some kind.

He had felt and now felt no physical fear at all. A commanding sense of power took him.

What was that soft thing under one foot? Oh. His hat. Don't shed objects like hats anywhere near this house.

It was nice after years of being kicked around, shoved, and

stepped on (old-timer) not to be worried about, Where do I go from here?

He had the answer to that question, he thought.

It was very clear and very simple.

Or so, at the time, it seemed to him.

NINE

De Lima ate his Sunday morning deviled kidneys, cooked and served by his cherished live-in English housekeeper, Mrs. Mount, with less than his usual satisfaction. His breakfast was taken in the little blue morning parlor of a high-ceilinged six-room apartment over the gallery, decorated by himself in ringing perfection throughout.

Blast that Smith/Landis girl. In spite of the blue eyes and the hair ribbon, she had given him an impression of the staying power of an ox.

After breakfast he called his lawyer, Thomas Pompton. "Sorry to disturb your Sabbath, but offhand can you tell me what if any rights illegitimate issue have, in the matter of inheritance of property, in the state of Maine?"

"Offhand," Pompton said indignantly, "I can't." He had just been leaving his apartment for a game of tennis at the River Club. "But I'll riffle through a book or two, in my library here, and if I can't put my finger on anything I'll call you from the office tomorrow."

"Tomorrow might be a little late," de Lima prodded delicately. As the gallery business was worth a good deal of money annually to Pompton & Corne, Pompton swore to himself, peeled off his white cable-knit sweater, and went to work. He called de Lima after twenty minutes of riffling.

"The Maine probate code's been revised recently. Under the

new code, kindred of the blood have the right of inheritance. There would of course have to be proof. Until the revision, the parent of the illegitimate issue had to acknowledge the relationship before a justice of the peace or—"

"That doesn't help us, does it," de Lima said. "But thank you anyway." There were two kinds of publicity, good and bad. That one, that wench, wouldn't sit on her hands for five years waiting to advance her claim in the courts. Spotlight of the press on John Swain, dawning realization that while he had been thought indubitably dead and gone, the law considered him legally alive for five years, in the state of Maine. Question: Was it, then, possible that he was?

A little chill wind blowing on the ardor of collectors. A wind that might gather and gust before the really big Swain headliner, the show of thirty new canvases in January.

De Lima had already started work on his news release. ". . . a treasury of magnificent recent work discovered in a locked loft in Swain's Bride's Bay barn . . ."

There was no indecency that people wouldn't get up to, or sit down to, in the courts. Especially when in the hands, as the girl might well be, of a scurrilous lawyer.

The money from Swain's pictures locked up for five years—but his dealer's commissions available immediately and legally to said dealer. There might be a vicious attempt to lay hands on some of this impressive sum. With demands to see the contract entitling him to 30 percent of the sale price of each picture.

The most recent agreement between the two men had been signed five years ago. On the back of it Swain had written, "I call this grand larceny, Adrian, but what's my alternative? Go peddle the stuff on street corners along with the people selling umbrellas and mechanical monkeys?" It was Swain's way, Swain's sharp tongue, and de Lima had thought nothing of the scrawl at the time. Artists, heaven bless them, couldn't be expected to express themselves like men of grayer professions.

"I call this grand larceny." What a marvelous handle for the thrusting, backstairs lawyer de Lima had already conjured up in his mind. Commissions put in escrow until . . . until years . . . until forever, while the fight went on.

And that grotesque puzzle. "She said she was his cousin

once removed but she's actually his daughter." What unspeakable machinations, under the shield of a false name,
might Johanna Landis be up to? Would she be afraid that
something would be done about her—done *to* her—if she
entered the affair under her own colors? But then that would
suggest that she knew or suspected something not quite right
about the death, the drowning—Impossible

There is no point, my dear fellow, de Lima said to himself,
in driving yourself crazy about everything all at once. Why not
see if this who's-who question could be cleared up right away?

He put on a dark gray suit, selected from his rack a walnut
walking stick, and went out with every appearance of church-
going splendor into the sunny October morning.

Johanna was wakened at nine by a call from her mother,
who had just gotten back from a month's visit to her sister,
Grace, in California. "I just thought," said Chloe Landis,
"*one* call about your father, and that would be that. Rest in
peace, and so on. It's just as well he's only a name to you. I
suppose out of sheer curiosity I will go and see his show. And
to think I told him he was better at teaching art than actually
doing it. Although all sorts of peculiar things these days are
called art. I can't help wondering who will get all that staggering money that seems to be involved."

"Someone named Maggie Lind," Johanna said. "A close
friend, I gather."

"It *would* be a woman," Chloe said tartly. "Well, dear, enjoy your Sunday, although I suppose hair washing and all
those tiresome things one has to do to get ready to go to work
on Monday . . ."

It was this call that caused her visitor to arrive unan-
nounced. She had decided not to go back to sleep, got up, put
on a creamy Mexican cotton robe, and was drinking her coffee
in a suitably washed and brushed if barefooted state when the
doorbell rang.

"Your line was busy," Sam Hines said. "I'd just come in at
Grand Central, and as you're so near I thought I'd pay you a
call."

"You're an early traveler. Have some coffee?"

"Yes, thanks. I was up all night, or most of it, at Nyack,

and I'm on my way home to get some sleep."

Who, or what, was at Nyack to keep him up all night?

"You look remarkably well for an all-night fling."

"Not a party—I've jumped over the edge of the cliff into a musical comedy. I never did one before. Jesse Tighe, who's doing the book, lives up there."

Propped against the long sill running under the casement windows, drinking his coffee, he looked contained, relaxed. Why then was the apartment exploding with him? Of course, it was a small apartment.

He put his cup down. "I hope and assume Alice isn't concealed somewhere on the premises?" He came over to her, took her hand, and pulled her lightly to her feet.

The telephone rang. Roger Gavin said, "I'm just leaving now. The basket's all packed, you don't have to bring a thing. I seem to remember that you like smoked salmon sandwiches."

"Will you give me, oh, half an hour, Roger? I've got a bit of unexpected company and I'm not quite organized. Dressed."

"You've got a good deal more than company," Sam said, from a few feet away. He moved, put his arms around her from behind, and kissed the nape of her neck. At her faint startled sound Roger said, "What's wrong, Johanna?"

"Not a thing. See you soon."

The doorbell rang again. "Alice, no doubt," said Sam, releasing her.

Jack Feroni was, as well as the unit producer she worked for, a near neighbor on East Thirty-eighth Street. He strode confidently in. The knowing lens of his eye went from Johanna in her creamy robe to the coffee cups on the windowsill to Sam, standing near the velvet-covered bed. A man who made a specialty of what in his view was a with-it crudeness, he put out a hand to Sam. "Congratulations. You've succeeded in what I've been trying to swing for years."

Sam coolly accepted the handshake. "Thank you."

"Well, dear," turning to Johanna, "now that everybody's up and at least some of us are dressed, I'm on my way to the office to see the rough cut of your San Francisco job. I thought you might like to come along."

"Sam Hines, Jack Feroni—my leader," Johanna said. "Thank you but I can't, I'm off for a picnic with Roger."

"That's the girl, off with the Hines, on with the Gavin." He gave Sam a sharp studying look. "Hines. Hines. Oh. If you're thinking of writing a song about her, forget it, it's been done long ago. 'When Johanna Loved Me.' See you tomorrow then, ducks. If I'd known you could keep all these balls in the air at once I would have and will try harder."

When the door closed behind him, Sam said, "I think we must find you another employer." He looked quietly outraged. His examining eyes were troubling.

Who and what was this girl, really, in her pretty undress? A musing on his part not pleasant to read. Unless she imagined it.

"It's unsatisfactory to offer a secondhand apology, but I do apologize for him," she said, a sudden lift to her head. "His vocabulary is part of my job. Surely the music business isn't all pink and white, and bows and curtsies?"

"No. And is it only his vocabulary you have to put up with? Can you pass him in the corridor without getting your thigh pinched?"

She flushed. "When you're a woman and you work with men, a lot of them, you grow a sort of hide, unattractive I suppose but necessary. Either that or you run screaming back to home and mother."

"So I've heard, but it's another thing to see it happening under my nose, and to you." He moved a restless hand. "Who may I ask is Roger Gavin?"

"He has the same job as Jack. Unit producer at UBC."

"Same style of man?"

"No. Quite proper and"—finding herself angry out of all proportion at being put on the carpet in this way—"very sweet."

He sighed. "As you've given me a time limit, I'll revert to the business at hand. I chased Maggie to your father's retrospective and crashed my way in." He repeated the brief exchange he and Maggie had had before Matt gave her opportunity for grateful escape.

Looking at her clouded face, he said, "Now see here, Johanna. Whatever he's up to, whatever they're up to, if this

isn't all mad—I suggest you close the book. He's literally dead
to the world and for the sake of my own sanity, if I were you, I
would give him a private second burial and then forget the
whole thing."

"You're really saying that you think this is all a publicity
stunt, a giant fraud, to jack up the prices of his work?"

"I wish I were more innocent, but, yes. To be fair, he could
be hiding from something or someone. I'll take that back—it
would only give you another bone to gnaw on." He looked at
his watch. "And now I'll leave you to your pleasures."

He sounded formal. Did he mean that in a final way? Over a
sinking sensation, she said, "Well, thank you for catching me
up. I'll try in future to follow your advice."

At the door he turned, eyebrows raised. "That has all the
earmarks of a long-term goodbye. What I meant is that I'll
leave you to your present pleasures until tomorrow. Mind you
keep Monday for me, Johanna."

Walking to the elevator, he met Adrian de Lima coming
up the hall. "Good morning," de Lima said. "You do get
around, Sam."

"So do you." Sam stopped and waited while the other man
pressed Johanna's doorbell. Then he went back up the hall to
stand behind de Lima for the door's opening. "I forgot my
cigarettes."

"Just a second, Roger," said her voice near the door. "I'm
only halfway into something."

De Lima, braced, looked with astonishment at Swain in the
feminine, Swain set to music. A slender limber young woman
in camel-colored pants and a yellow pullover sweater which
had left her hair shiningly tousled.

He ignored Sam's unnerving, guardian presence close behind him. "I am sorry. I see"—stepping back a pace to check
her door number and just missing Sam's foot—"you are 4G. I
had wanted 5G. My apologies." He turned and walked away,
swinging his walnut stick.

Sam decided there was no point in worrying her unnecessarily until he had given a little thought to what this mistaken
door number might be all about. If anything.

"Goodbye again," he said. "Until, off with the Gavin and
on with the Hines."

Under the sidewalk canopy he passed a man on his way in. About his own age, tall, fair, blue-eyed, with a country or rather a country-house freshness about him.

He's quite proper and very sweet.

I think, Sam told himself, that under the circumstances—all of them—Jesse and I will switch our working operations from Nyack to New York.

TEN

It never hurts to know exactly who your victim is.

On Sunday, at a little after noon, Matt called Helena Coe in Philadelphia and found her at home. He had gotten her winter address by a telephone call to a real estate agent. "This is Joseph Green with the county clerk's office."

"On Sunday?" she inquired sharply.

"Overtime," Matt said mournfully. "We're as usual way behind. I'm making a tabulation of the winter population at Seashell Park. Now, is your house tenanted?"

"Yes, thank God. Is that all?"

"If you'd just give me your tenant's name, age, occupation, length of lease . . . we'll be shuttling some of this information to the Chamber of Commerce so that—"

Hearing the rustle of red tape, she reported impatiently, "Name, John Wright. I don't know his exact age. Fifties I'd say. Retired insurance man. He's taken the house until the end of next May."

"Thank you for your cooperation. Have a nice day."

Turning yourself into an actually nonexistent John Wright cut both ways, Matt thought. After your death, there was no way to place you in time and space, no home, no past, no friends, no enemies, no connections of any kind. Nothing to go on. You were dead. But there wasn't any you to die.

Period.

Maggie would know who the dead *you* was. Maggie with real grief and loss to handle.

Maggie alone now, really alone. Maggie needing his help, his support, his love. Really needing him.

Knowing he wouldn't be able to show himself in the town by daylight, he had brought along delicatessen sandwiches in his duffle bag, and several candy bars, along with the gun.

He did, savagely, miss his morning coffee. Seeing him at the telephone in the lounge, Mrs. Paglieri said, "I didn't hear you go out this morning, could you use a cup of coffee?"

"Yes, thanks—I'll take it up to my room."

"Not going out to enjoy our beautiful fresh air and sun and ocean?"

"I'm really here for a rest. Very comfortable room. And I've got the window wide open. I'll be checking out some time tonight, depending on when my friend can pick me up. We may as well settle up now, in case you're asleep." He paid her a modest twelve fifty in cash.

He wasn't entirely sure why he had brought along the gun. Maybe in anticipated self-defense, if his quarry got onto him rather than the other way around? Swain was a formidable man, tough, fit, and under these circumstances could be considered mortally dangerous to encounter. Yes, that must be why he had brought it with him.

It was an old well-oiled Colt .32. It had been his father's. Pawn whatever, he had never pawned the gun. In a world where he had always felt surrounded by hostility, it was a reliable if silent friend. As a young man he had belonged to the East Side Gun and Target Club and while he hadn't target-practiced for years felt the sure eye and hand would come readily to his aid. If needed.

The afternoon was long. He read, ate a ham and cheese sandwich, the Swiss cheese gone limp and oily, tried to nap, and occasionally went to the window to look down into Ocean Boulevard. A few strollers, mostly elderly. A few cars, of makes and years that he described to himself as lower-middle-class. What a place to be in, at forty-eight years of age—Mrs. Paglieri's boardinghouse in Seashell Park, New Jersey.

But right around the corner the past was waiting to be picked up. He lay on his daffodiled bed, shoes off, somewhere between waking and sleeping.

He and Maggie, fun, drinks, laughter, and all right, a fight or two, Maggie's magnificent food, party Sundays, opinions being shouted all over the room. New York, that other New York and not shabby West Fourteenth Street, and a month now and then in Provincetown, they both loved Provincetown. She might have to wait for her big money, but one way or another she was never without some money of her own. (That Landis girl's indignant denial of any idea of a court suit. Really, Maggie, you sweet bitch. But your Matt knows how to deal with your little stratagems.)

At eight o'clock, he put on his raincoat and his hat, dropped the gun into the inside pocket of the raincoat, drank a double shot of whiskey, his first all day, and went out into the dusk-darkness. He had noted the night before an empty house directly across the street from Swain's. He went up the connecting short street, Atlantic Avenue, toward Parade Street, and slipped past the back of a dully lighted corner house to his empty stucco cube of a dwelling. There was a carport at one side, open at either end, beautifully protecting, even supplying an immense red kerosene drum, handy if and when he wanted to crouch and hide from passing car headlights.

He had no exact plan, not knowing Swain's evening habits. But that didn't disturb him. Play it loose. Play it by ear. And relax.

There were lights on in Helena Coe's house. At eight-thirty, the screened porch door opened and Swain, in an unlikely-looking city-bred topcoat, came out and down the two steps. He gave no impression of indecision, of wondering where he was going to take himself. He turned right on Parade Street to the near corner. Then he turned the corner and headed toward the sea.

Matt emerged from his mothering carport and followed him, silently sneakered, at a discreet distance, prepared to whisk himself off the sidewalk and behind a house if Swain looked back. But he didn't. His stride was brisk and free, purposeful, and somehow suggested a habit, a walk done daily, not on an errand but for pleasure.

He crossed Ocean Boulevard, and then the last wide street parallel with the boardwalk and the sea. The boardwalk was broad, twelve feet or so, and from where Matt paused behind a garage seemed to go on forever in either direction. Penny-pinching of energy evident: only one in every four or five of the boardwalk lamp standards was lighted, so that there were long dark stretches. The sea threw up a faint brilliance, but it was more shine than light. Directly ahead of him there was a wooden sun shelter on the boardwalk where the burned and blistered could huddle in the summer. With luck, there would be more shelters.

Swain on reaching the boardwalk turned right, going north. Matt availed himself rapidly of the sun shelter. Swain lost for a while, then there he was again, under a distant lamp, perhaps a hundred yards away.

Matt left the boardwalk, crossed the wide street, and walked north on the cracked sidewalk. If Swain looked back, what would he see? Another chap who liked a walk near the ocean before tucking in for a good night's sleep. A short man in a concealing hat and raincoat, another good fast walker.

The next lighted lamp standard sketched on the farthest reaches of its irradiation a confusing, at first, loom of walls, towers, terraces. Almost totally dark, the great loom. Matt finally identified it as the situation on the boardwalk where the big hotels and motels and restaurants gathered in a flock. Closed, all of them, with or without night watchmen, considering the price of help and the cost of burglary-prevention devices. Be careful: police patrol cars might be dutiful in checking all this invested money.

The complex of large buildings was now between him and Swain. He would have to get onto, or close to, the boardwalk. He crossed the street and found a shelter handily waiting. From within it he strained his eyes to the limits of dimmest visibility: the boardwalk disappearing, just night and beach and water. No, it had probably turned a sharp curve, Swain continuing around the curve, lost from sight and sound. But he would have to come back. Unless he chose another route home?

A faintest, distant footfall to the north, and a startling sound, a gay whistling. "In Dublin's fair city, where girls are so pretty . . ."

Matt started violently at a whirring from behind him. He huddled deeper into the shadows of the shelter. A bicyclist, a dauntless elderly woman with wild flying gray hair, speeding down the center of the boardwalk. *Christ*—an accidental bodyguard for Swain. She braked about twenty yards beyond the shelter, got off her bicycle, and stood at the edge of the boardwalk doing, evidently, deep-breathing exercises. She got back on her bicycle after three or four minutes, after forever, and began rapidly pedaling past Matt in the opposite direction, south. Bodyguard removing herself. God speed you, Matt thought, out of a sweating waking nightmare. Funny kind of thought, when you took a look at it.

Now.

Swain entering the farthest edge of the light, heading back. The point is, not to think about it, just let your hand do the thinking.

With one knee braced against the corner of a bench, because his whole body had begun to shake, Matt waited. Another ten yards—

He took careful aim and pulled the trigger of his Colt. The crash sounded like a lifetime (his)—a universe exploding. Through a haze somewhere near a faint, he saw Swain plunge over the edge of the boardwalk. Not far away he heard a car's engine. Police patrol car? Would they have heard the sound of the shot? He was about thirty yards away from the first of the hotel buildings. He ran, not even taking time to look to his left—down where Swain was lying—and found a great curving concrete wing around an empty swimming pool at the rear of the hotel. He crouched in near-total darkness behind the wing. He waited in agony for screams of pain. Or the sight of Swain's head, Swain risen from the dead, twice, appearing above the edge of the boardwalk. Nothing. Silence. Except for the sound of the engine, fading away south.

Get the hell out of here. He moved in the darkness in the direction of what he thought was the street, feeling his way along rough concrete, interspersed with the glass of what must be huge windows.

Now, a beckoning glow from a streetlight. It showed him a paved terrace opening up ahead, some kind of summer dining place at the side of a hotel, the metal bones of awning supports casting shadows on the flagstones. He ran across the terrace and around to stand trembling under the broad marquee in front.

No cars coming in either direction. Across the street, scrub and long grass, a few stunted trees, no houses. The sidewalk must have ended a block or so back. He took a fast plunge into this miniature wilderness and half-ran, brambles tearing at his trousers, until he reached the street right-angled to the sea where the interminable houses began again.

Just walk, but fast. Hands in pockets. Man taking night air. Not that anyone was likely to see him. One out of every three or four houses with lights in them. Shades mostly drawn. Thundering heart in the man going by, but nobody but he could hear his heart.

Now the hard part. Or the next hardest. He couldn't afford to be reported by Mrs. Paglieri, if questions were asked by the police about strangers in town, as having returned to the house at, by his watch, eight forty-eight, when at about eight-thirty a man named Wright had been shot on the boardwalk.

He went back to his carport, sat down on the cement floor huddled behind the kerosene drum, taking care to put a newspaper down first from a pile against the wall; it wouldn't do to risk grease stains on the seat of his pants. He waited half an hour.

The house across the street (a fringe benefit, if you liked to call it that, able to be under observation from his enforced hiding place) remained silent, dark. Dead.

He got up, replaced the newspaper on its pile, and returned, strolling, to the Dory Dune. Mrs. Paglieri had given him a key. He let himself in without surreption. She appeared in a plaid bathrobe at the top of the stairs. "Well, you did get out after all, Mr. Matthews."

"Only to a smoke-filled room," Matt said with a grin. "My friend with his car turned up and we went to play a little poker with a friend of *his*. I'll be leaving in ten minutes or so, I'll make sure the door's locked. Don't be surprised if you see me again. Nice place you've got."

"Goodnight then. Happy trip to—?"

"Philadelphia," said Matt.

He walked a mile and a half by the shore road to the next town down the coast, Parkersville, and at a little after ten o'clock checked into a motel offering twenty-four-hour service. He signed the register card "Thomas Walker." He winked at the girl behind the counter. "All alone tonight."

"Well, cheer up," she said. "There's worse things than having nothing to do but sleep."

ELEVEN

The bullet had just nicked the top of Swain's ear but for a while he didn't know that.

First the instinctive hurling himself off the boardwalk, into the sand, then the animal crawling, scrambling, underneath the boardwalk. Hand to his neck, wet. He couldn't see his hand but the skin informed him of what was smearing it and running down his neck.

The wild questioning hand went to his head. Hair thick. *Dry*. Then where, what . . . ? Fingers shrinking from their dreadful exploration of another mortal entry, at the nape, through the side of his forehead?

He was still face down in the sand. It gritted in his teeth and on his tongue. As his hand moved, his elbow touched a discarded soft-drink can and it clinked against another can. The little metallic sound seemed to him like the crashing of cymbals. He stiffened with terror and stopped breathing for a moment or so. Was the man directly above him, or near, waiting to see if the treatment had worked? Ears cocked, along with the gun?

All he could hear was the chuckle and whisper of the incoming tide. He began slowly, deeply, to breathe again.

Elbow pressed against his side so as not to knock into anything else, he continued probing. Neck all right. Forehead all right, although wet with an innocent and recognizable fluid lighter than blood. Eyes? He blinked and felt firm surfaces under his lids. Nothing hurt, but that didn't mean anything. Shocked flesh waiting to deliver its message. Ear?

Yes. At the top of the flange of his right ear, there wasn't the usual incurved-petal feeling but a squashy softness. In new terror, he put his little finger in his ear, heard the rustle of skin against skin, but felt no pain and no moisture.

It seemed, incredibly, that he was all right. Nicked, nothing else. *But.* In its held-in hysteria, his mind found a phrase from the past, something that aunts and mothers said.

It's the thought that counts.

Someone had thought to kill him, had tried, and had failed. This time. Until when? ten minutes, a half hour from now? Someone waiting, or crawling underneath the opposite side of the boardwalk, feeling his way for his prey to see if he were dead or alive? No. There was no slightest sound, and his recovering night vision showed him cans and paper cups, crumpled paper bags, stretching away in a broad ribbon on either side of him. "Don't bother with the litter can, dear, you'll get lost. Just throw it under the boardwalk."

Near at hand he saw a handsome piece of litter: a croquet mallet. People did play croquet on the hard sand flats when the tide was full out. Flung far away in a rage at a missed shot, perhaps. It provided arms of a kind, better than nothing, and the nearby small rustle of a rat decided him on movement. He must have been here, in the sea-breathing silence, for fifteen minutes or so. He got himself out from underneath the boardwalk and crawled on hands and knees along it, close, to the next lamp standard up. Then he raised his head slightly, and saw nothing but the empty eye-level boards. He resumed his crawl. Farther up, where there was very little light, and a large parking place with no concealing houses across the street where a man with a gun could wait patiently, he darted, bent, across the boardwalk and the parking lot. He was now not far from his house.

A killer would be more hesitant, wouldn't he, shooting at a man in front of or near a house with lights in it? People rushing out, or those too frightened to come out reaching for the telephone and calling the police? Don't run, though. A running man in the night might be enough to terrify a house-holder into a police alarm.

Not his own house. The hand with the gun might be quietly waiting there. He left the sidewalk and cut left, to the back of Ada Garble's house. Her garage behind made an ell which provided total concealment from his premises. A light on, thank Christ, in the kitchen.

Stop and think for a moment. Don't get her excited, don't tell her what happened, or she would lose all her usefulness. He tapped very lightly against the curtained glass pane in the upper half of her kitchen door. It opened at once. She made an O of her mouth to show delighted surprise, and he said, "Ssshhh. Couple of old biddies going by. They'll suspect the worst." He slipped in as her eyes widened in horror at what must be a considerable amount of blood from the little, life-saving nick in the ear.

"Tricycle left on the boardwalk. I tripped in the dark and fell off and scraped my ear on the rough edge," explained Swain. "I thought you might be kind enough to bandage it for me."

"You look white, you look faint, sit down quick." She pulled out a kitchen chair. The shade, he noticed, was tight to the sill. She came back in a moment with bandaging and disin-fectant. "Wash it first, how could an ear bleed so?" She talked soothingly as she ran water into a bowl. "Better in no time though." As if to divert him from excruciating pain, she chattered on.

"Turn your head a bit toward the light . . . I remembered this afternoon who I thought you were. My sister worked at St. Elizabeth's Academy in Morristown. She was sick in bed and I went over to give a hand. We were both young then. She was a—an assistant housekeeper. I did the beds for a couple of days, beds for forty girls in my dorm, no joke, I tell you." She touched a cotton ball dipped in disinfectant to his ear. "Don't stiffen so, this doesn't hurt, it isn't iodine. Well, one rainy day, I was coming down the steps with my arms full of slept-in sheets. I tripped and would have fallen but a man coming up the stairs caught me. That's why I always remembered his face because for a second I thought I'd break my neck for sure. He

went on up and I went on down and later I wanted to thank
him but he was in class and I had to leave that afternoon. John
Swain, his name was, I found out from my sister—from my
description of him. Taught art. She said all the girls were crazy
about him. I meant to send him a note but never did. Isn't that
the way of things? There, nice-looking bandage if I say so
myself. Yes, if John Swain has a double, you're it. Of course
the hair—his was—well, he was young. Shiny, falling around
a little—and beautiful eyes, I'll never forget his eyes."

Swain had remembered to put on his dark glasses at her
back door. Feeling very cold, he shrugged his shoulders with
invalid impatience. "Art," he said. "I wish I knew how to
draw, I could illustrate my own shells and birds and things."

"He had the same eyebrows as you do too."

He couldn't bear her eyes this close. "Could you get me
some aspirin please." Would she be on the phone tomorrow
telling her friends about the man next door who looked like
John Swain? Had she been on it already? When would one of
them pick up the name—"Swain? He's a famous artist. He
drowned not so long ago. I saw it in the paper."

But eyes or no, he still needed her. He said, getting up
slowly, "I'd be best off home. But you've been so kind. Will
you come along with me and have a drink? To celebrate"—he
couldn't help the hard mirthless curve of his mouth—"my
escape from the grave?"

"I'd love to." Pleased with the opportunity of playing
nurse and comforter to this elusive man, she beamed. Outside
the back door, he took her arm. Natural that a man weakened
with loss of blood would feel the need of a little support.

*If you're here, waiting for me, you'd never shoot the two of
us together.*

His key opened the deck door into silence. Faint smell of
turpentine, his own special life-giving ozone; he had done a
few forbidden small oil sketches this afternoon, ideas he
wanted to get down before he lost them. (Maggie had smug-
gled to him, under protest, the beginner's set of oils. "Don't
worry, I promise you it will be an entirely private vice. And
what use would I be to any of us in future if I went stark staring mad here?") He had hidden the sketches before leaving the
house under Helena Coe's stack of a year's worth of *New*

Yorkers in one corner of the living room.

Switching on the kitchen light, he stood looking around indecisively. "Now where would I have put my bottle? On a shelf somewhere. Are you good at finding things?"

A man with a gun under a bed. In a closet. Behind a door.

"You sit down, I'll poke around. Your bedroom maybe?"

"I just have this recollection of putting it on a shelf . . ."

Cravenly, cannily, as he put it to himself, he sat at the table while she roamed the house, turning on lights as she went, enjoying the satisfaction of curiosity, the invitation to invade his privacy. Poor lamb, bed not made. She came back empty-handed and he said, "I've just remembered. The cabinet under the sink."

It was scotch, at which she wrinkled her nose. "Oh, that always tastes like medicine. But that's what you need, medicine!" and she laughed happily. She poured herself a small drink and him a large one. He disposed of it in two gulps. She eyed the glass doubtfully and then poured another inch and a half. "Don't suppose you can come to much harm this near your own bed. Would you mind if I made up the bed for you? More comfortable that way."

"No thanks." Weariness was not hard to assume; he let his shoulders sag. "You've been very kind. I think soon I'll get into that rabbit's burrow . . ."

But in a way he was sorry to see her close the back door behind her. Because now there was nothing to do but walk head on into the dark unknown. There was nothing to do but think.

If the bullet had personal intentions, they could not be for John Wright because there was no John Wright.

A random purpose-without-purpose shot, some young thug minded to pick off any moving target?

A momentarily comforting if staggering view of what the United States had come to: a shooting gallery without rival anywhere in the world.

If not some aimlessly roving bucket of hatred ready to empty itself, who?

Who had taken near deadly aim at eminent American artist John Swain's head?

Who?

De Lima? *Good Christ.*

Maggie? *Never.*

Both? Heads together, whispers, a recently thought of or long-laid plan. All right, don't run from this unthinkable idea. Sit with it, look at it. Someone tried to kill you.

There would never be anything to connect either of them with the sudden violent death of an insurance man in an unfashionable town in New Jersey.

The deed could be done with impunity. Tempting, if you took a good cold look at it. Maggie his heir, even though she'd have to wait a while. De Lima, who a week ago had grossed for himself in commissions approximately three hundred thousand dollars. And with thirty pictures still to go.

But why would de Lima want to kill him? Some kind of split arranged between them? Go back to that later.

Insane ramblings, these. Delayed shock taking over, skewing his brain so that he saw everything slantwise or upside down. Or, like one of his own painted suggestions of disastrous flame under cool floating color.

A faint sound brought him to his feet. Fingers at a window latch? More probably a mouse.

Could he dare now or ever to go to bed? A muzzle against the bedroom windowpane, a hit-or-miss raking of bullets deep into the bedding, the mattress, and with luck into human flesh.

Unless it was all totally without point, his random wandering thug turning his attention to other atrocities. But how could you take this convenient shadowy theory for granted? To do so would be at the very real risk of your life.

Was he to sit here, or stand and stride here, waiting hour after hour, day after day, week after week, for extermination?

Swain's safely pinned down, my dear—trapped if you like.

He took a bleak look at trapped and terrified John Swain. Living here in forced isolation. Turning himself into a recluse, suspicious of every sound, windows locked, doors locked, not daring to go out of the house by day or night.

What for instance would he do about groceries? There was only one store open and they didn't deliver. What would he do about—?

Impossible. The thing to do, the only thing, was to pack up and get out. Remove the black center disc from the target. But—and the realization fell thuddingly—he couldn't. The bank in Bride's Bay would by now have secured his account, holding it intact until the law released it to his heir. His only income was provided by de Lima, paid semimonthly into the Seashell Park First Trust Bank, the checks arranged to be drawn against his own present and future earnings. The deposits were from the Chemical Bank of New York. Swain vaguely remembered that checks to him in the past were from the Bank of New York. So that, he thought, there was nothing even in bank records to connect de Lima with John Wright.

Speaking of banks, a matter of balancing. Practical daily dollars, as against his continued existence.

His continued existence, that is, as John Wright.

He was damned if he was going to die for John Wright.

First, a necessary investigation by telephone. He dialed Maggie's number at the Barclay, was put through to her room and got no answer. Only ten-something on Sunday night, out enjoying herself somewhere. But no, she couldn't be seen enjoying herself. She would have to be wearing her dramatic dark cloak of grief.

Or was she not there because she was on her way back by car from Seashell Park? He put a finger to the bandage on his ear. A faint throbbing had begun underneath it.

Next. De Lima's number. "Hello," said the rich ripe voice, adding unnecessarily, "De Lima here."

The first thought that flicked across Swain's racing mind was that if de Lima wanted him dead for some reason there were men who could be hired for such tasks. In the context of pure survival, de Lima's presence at home was not a guarantee of innocence.

Swain's fear and rage rose and almost choked him. "Someone a little while back tried to kill me," he said. "Shoot me. I'm afraid our romp has come to an early end. As of about a minute from now, Adrian, I am John Swain. Recovered—by another near miss—from his amnesia."

TWELVE

At first de Lima could plainly and simply not believe his ears.

What madness was this, on top of the afternoon, on top of Alice Smith?

"You could get yourself murdered," Stan said to Alice on Sunday morning.

"Not in a public place, not with people around," Alice said serenely. "Where's a nice public place in New York, Stan, where you can have a quiet talk?"

Over toasted corn muffins, Stan gave the matter his attention. "Paley Park ought to do. The waterfall'd cover up what you're talking about. Maybe I should go to this meeting to—uh—see you're protected." She had been evasive about what she wanted to meet the gallery man for. ". . . oh, just to remind him I'm around, and that I won't be dropping this. He's the trustee. He's going to have to deal with me one way or the other." To his offer to accompany her to Paley Park, "I don't think so. I mean, you're a stranger. I'm one of the family. But being your day off you can drive me in and wait somewhere, I'm sick of that old train."

She had typed a memory-perfect transcript of the conversation overheard in de Lima's office. This she put into her handbag along with a small square of cardboard in a protective

138

envelope. She called de Lima's apartment number four times and when she reached him at noon said, "Would you meet me this afternoon at three-thirty in Paley Park, Mr. de Lima?"

"Certainly not. Who is this? Miss Smith?"

"Well then, seeing you can't make it, I'll just go to the newspapers. With my picture and my telephone call written down, that I heard at your show."

The newspapers. What telephone call? A picture of whom? Questions would indicate weakness. Meeting her would show anxiety, vulnerability—guilt. Or would it? "Look here, Miss Smith, I can't have these gnats around my head. I've just thought, I'm due in Sutton Place at five and I have a busy afternoon before that. I can give you ten minutes at say twenty minutes to five. By my watch." Reins back in his hands; just enough bored impatience in his voice to make her catch her lower lip in her white eyetooth.

William S. Paley's pocket-park gift to the City of New York, on East Fifty-third Street, was lilac-shadowed when Alice got there, buildings on either side blocking the late slanting sun. Stan had been right. The water rushing down the high rear wall made quite a commotion. She seated herself in a white metal chair at a table under a young tree, and to have something to do until Mr. de Lima showed up—if he did show up—nibbled on a peppermint cream.

There were three or four other people, two of them playing cards at a table. They looked at her incuriously, even though, thought Alice, I look quite nice. Pink-and-white-checked jersey suit, pink ribbon to hold back her hair.

People did look up when de Lima arrived; he projected an air of definitely being someone. A woman reading the New York *Times Book Review* put him down as United Nations, perhaps, with that olive skin, from some oil country. God knows they made enough money to dress the way he did.

De Lima brushed the seat of the chair beside Alice's with his handkerchief and sat down. "Now then, young woman?" He looked a little amused, eyebrows raised, as if wondering what he was doing here.

She opened her handbag. "First, what I heard that woman in black saying over the telephone in your office. I mean, she must have been talking to John Swain, mustn't she? 'Right now, two women are having a bloody battle over you.' I'm so thrilled he's *alive*, but of course I can't help wondering."

De Lima read the transcript slowly. His face showed no sign of the turmoil in his heart and veins. With a boxer's instinct to go after the opponent while he was doubled over and groaning—and she thought he must be, inside him—Alice got out the envelope and slipped from it the small oil dashed down on a square of cardboard. A sketch, tender and swift, of a young woman sitting on the edge of a bathtub bending over to dry one foot with a blue towel.

"Not everybody likes showing pictures of their mother with no clothes on," Alice said. "But it does show what you'd call, intimacy, doesn't it? Turn it over."

On the back, the familiar scrawling hand. "Darling Ellie—after love *with* love, John Swain."

"She gave this to my aunt to hide, naturally she didn't want my stepfather to find it," Alice explained helpfully. She sat back and waited with pleasure to see what this high-and-mighty man might do now.

Would his voice work? Yes, it did. "As to the phone call, it cannot automatically be ruled out. But as near you what that means is a third person, to whom she was speaking, had put in an early bid on that particular picture, 'Number Seventy-one.' " He couldn't see the phone call bearing any weight legally or with, God in heaven, the police. But what a terrific time the newspapers she had waved in his face would have with it. "IS DEAD ARTIST ALIVE?"

One last wisp of canniness remained to him in the dark chasm into which he had stumbled and fallen hard. Force *her* to make the extortion demand. "What exactly did you have in mind, with these bits and pieces?"

"I thought you might want to give me some money, in advance, before it's proved that I have a right to the—the other money." She was unblushing, blue eyes clear and bright.

"Do you realize, my dear, that what you're proposing is a criminal offense for which you could be prosecuted and imprisoned?" De Lima took out a small gold snuffbox, placed a pinch in his left nostril, and sniffed. This gesture could unnerve simple people.

Used to Mr. Berlin's money maneuvers, Alice said, "You could list it as a business expense. And of course I'd deny I ever said any such things to you. I don't know all that much about art but if a man's dead and can't paint anymore, then people would pay higher prices, wouldn't they. If he's alive, though . . ."

Get out of this fast. Too dangerous, and rage was blotting out his wits, the fabled win-every-hand de Lima wits.

"I've explained why you misunderstood the call. And I have just a minute or two left for you." Say nothing that couldn't be quoted. "I might be interested in your little sketch. Examples of Swain's figure work are quite rare. Even though it's on cardboard—Suppose we settle on our plan. I must fly off to Paris tonight." Untrue, but she couldn't know that and might be impressed. She was; she nodded. Arrange for a chunk of time: something was going to have to be done about this frightful hair-ribboned girl. He saw months, years of harassment, threats, a deadly poisoned nibbling at his exposed heel. "I'll be back, let's see, on Thursday. Bring your little picture to my office and we'll discuss terms."

He had succeeded in momentarily puzzling and sidetracking Alice, but she registered very clearly the words "discuss terms."

With a cool "Good afternoon" he got up and left her. He headed east, where Sutton Place lay, if she chose to look suspiciously after him and if she had ever heard of Sutton Place. Then he went south on Lexington Avenue and back to his apartment.

He had turned more than one corner in his walk. He had set his feet on a path never before trodden, even in brink's-edge professional adventures.

Transfer any suggestion of hysteria to the other man; even though he himself had been feeling a little, frightening lick of it since this afternoon.

"One of us has to remain calm," de Lima said patiently to Swain, over the telephone. "Begin at the beginning, John."

"The beginning and very nearly the end," Swain said nakedly. "About eight-thirty on the boardwalk here, I was shot at. The bullet was an inch or so off and got the tip of my ear."

"You haven't," de Lima interrupted in horror, "gone to the police?"

"No. Or, not yet. I managed to get home and I'm locked in tight. But I will not live this way, Adrian, as said before, not a day longer. Or to put it more succinctly die this way. One year of my life down the drain, all right. But not, Jesus Christ, all of it and all at once."

"I am appalled," de Lima said. "Horrified. One hardly dares to venture out today, does one, even in the depths of New Jersey. I suppose some coked-up finger on the trigger of a stolen gun—but I know how you feel."

"Do you? Has anyone ever tried to kill you?"

"A bottle at the head once, but the man had several bottles inside him." His voice was soothing. "Let's talk in the morning, when you've had time to sleep away this unspeakable thing, and . . ."

Swain read the other man's mind. He was to be calmed like a frightened child and then when he was able to see reason he would arise with cool courage to face another John Wright day.

"I have too much to lose. I tell you, flatly and without any question, it's over."

There was a silence while de Lima considered what was unmistakably an ultimatum.

On the one hand, you have too much to lose, John.

And on the other hand, I have too much to lose.

"Look. Try to listen and try to *think*. You can't recover your wits under that name, in that role, in that place. I'd planned—for months from now—to get the staging right, the rehearsal, the location, the clothing, the story, everything."

Swain blew out his breath and emitted a reluctant, growling "Well . . ."

"You do see that, of course. You're going to have to give me at the very least a couple of days. A plan to be made, transport for you to be arranged. To say nothing of a reason for John Wright's temporarily leaving town—invented and documented—so that there won't be disastrous queries tagging along after you. Even if you think your man or person with the gun wants another pot at you, has a genuine reason for wanting you dead, promise me you'll sit tight, behind locked doors if that helps. Are you short of anything, food, drink, aspirin, liquor? I can have someone drive down early with a box of provisions. John Wright's aunt in Roslyn, Long Island, sending him some of her homemade jams and jellies and so on . . .''

John Wright did well and truly die when he went over the edge of the boardwalk, Swain thought grimly, but he refused to subject himself to further dosages of de Lima common sense.

"No, I have everything I need."

De Lima, who in his eggshell-walking had momentarily lost touch with firm earth, took this as agreement.

"Good. Give me Monday and Tuesday. I'll be in touch with you sometime on Wednesday." About to replace the receiver, he checked the little red button close to the mouthpiece. Had he pushed it in? He usually did, automatically, without thinking about it, when there was any suggestion of agitation, danger, trouble to his ear. Yes, he had. Swain was down on tape. For what that was worth.

If anything.

It was only after the call that Swain remembered Ada Garble's near-identification; but coming as it had after the evening's major event it had seemed only the distant flashing of a red light. But then, he wouldn't be here if and when a blurred recollection hardened into certainty. She had been kind and he wouldn't want to endanger her.

Endanger her?

Be careful about your mind. The threat of death around every bend.

He had turned out all the lights when she left and his only illumination was a flashlight set eight inches above the floor on a footstool. Don't offer the indoor shadow of a man looming, sketching himself on a drawn shade. Here is your target, and he is all alone.

He would wait another hour or so to call Maggie once more, to see if she was home from her evening. Or from Seashell Park.

He sat staring half-hypnotized by the round white eye of the flashlight, trying to search his past. An enemy? You had to have friends and acquaintances to develop real enemies, he thought ironically, and he had left those far behind in time. Some soured, mad student left over from the days of his Bride's Bay school, cherishing a hatred, carrying it around with him? Some woman he had ended an affair with, and who had never gotten over it? Or, the woman's husband? "If I ever lay eyes on that bastard again, I'll kill him."

Nonsense. Put away these beyond-the-limits rovings of a panicked mind.

But the bullet wasn't nonsense, nor the throbbing ear.

At a little before midnight he called the Barclay and got Maggie. First he asked casually where she had been all evening. Maggie said she'd gotten tired of not looking happy in front of other people so she had taken herself off to a movie where she could laugh out loud, and then gone to P.J. Clarke's for a cup of chili and a glass of wine.

Swain thought it could have been the truth or a marvelously sound alibi. He told her in three swift sentences about the murder attempt. At the second account of it, he sounded odd to himself, melodramatic. Poor Swain's gone a little stir crazy all by himself in Seashell Park. Some kid shooting at a seagull, some aelurophobe firing away at a cat.

Maggie said, "But—" and then stopped.

"But what?"

"They mightn't have been shooting at the insurance man, but at *you*. You've got to get out of there."

"I'm going to."

"Can I help?"

"No. If he knew *me*, of course he would know you, or about you. Adrian's working on it."

"Then you're in efficient if slippery hands. Where is he going to put you?"

"I have no idea." And, rapid second thought, If I knew it might be a little unwise to tell you. Which he tried to dismiss before he reminded himself that this particular time, survival time, was not the season to dismiss any qualm however disloyal. Not even to give Maggie a clean slate, Maggie with friends in every direction in Manhattan, among them her adored Sam Hines. Gregarious Maggie, who had gone off all by herself to a movie?

Think about sleep again? A hazardous idea. Here I am, buried in miles, distance, dreams, wholly at your mercy. Not hearing the tickle of sound at the door, at the window. Or the first thin crackling. And then the fire, helped along by kerosene, gathering power, the old salt-dried wooden house flaming up, burning down—

Charred body found, unidentifiable, but the tenant was said to be a John Wright, who . . .

He put the flashlight on the floor, its beam aimed at the kitchen, and went to get himself a drink of scotch. Light drink. Keep your head, although it no longer seemed capable of any useful work. Producing nothing but fantasies now.

Promise me you'll sit tight. Give me Monday and Tuesday.

Give me two days to dispose of you. *Really* dispose of you this time. Just stay where you are until I get myself organized, so that it can be done in such a way that no one will ever—

Round and round. De Lima the trustee, Maggie the heir, John Swain in legal limbo, neither living nor dead. Nowhere was where he was. But, by the light of any working intelligence, drowned.

Sit tight? No.

Listening to the rising wind at about four o'clock, he took out his wallet. A new wallet bought for him by de Lima and furnished with a snapshot in its plastic slip of his dead wife, Nora. Gray hair, glasses, the face shared by countless thousands of women, all, it seemed, wives.

He had fifty-seven dollars in the wallet. There had been a balance of a little over two hundred in the bank after he had paid his rent on October 1 and he had drawn several hefty checks since then, not liking standing at tellers' windows every day or so.

Had de Lima planned all along to keep him short so that there was no chance he could cut and run?

Run to whom?

Was there anyone in the world he could trust?

His fingers, nervously re-counting the bills, touched the edge of an envelope he had transferred from his battered old morocco billfold.

No one left to trust but himself. Or, at a wild and desperate tangent, that other self, looking at him across a room above the sea?

("I was just passing by on my way to Jonesport . . . I hate droppers-in myself."

("You have a rather readable face, Johanna.")

("Well. I must be on my way. It sounds odd in this context, but, nice to have met you.")

A stranger. But no matter how ill met and not deserved, his own.

The penciled phone number on the envelope was pale with rubbing, but still there.

The New York area code was, what? 212.

Just for a day or so. Until de Lima, by telephone and not in his possibly weaponed person, could satisfactorily explain his plans for summoning John Swain back to this sweet business of life.

THIRTEEN

"Monday begins at midnight," Sam Hines said into her ear, over the telephone.

Johanna smiled to herself in the near-darkness. She was in bed and had been half asleep. Lights from the brownstone houses across the back gardens gave her café curtains a faint pink glow.

"Is that a song of yours?"

"Not yet. It might be."

"You sound very much awake."

"I am. I had to see you were safely back from the woods and meadows. No bites? Or scratches?"

"Quite intact."

"I will now allow you a little sleep. But expect me around eight o'clock."

"That late?"

"I mean eight o'clock in the morning. I have just granted you the day off. It's a long time since the seventh of May, Johanna, we must not waste any more of it. I thought, a nice quiet interval with no interruptions this time, and perhaps a little champagne for breakfast. Then you will come with me to Long Island, to Quogue, where at my little house we will plant five dozen bulbs for spring. After that's done we can feel free to dally."

How unexpectedly French he sounded, not the accent but the phrasing. Was this always his manner when wooing?

And incidentally, was one of the reasons for this festive call to find out if she was now alone or still in the company of her fellow picnicker? She gave him back a "goodnight" as privately murmured as his own.

Lying thinking about him, about the morning, the day, was a little like Christmas and birthday eves rolled into one, the uneasy joys of expectation, surprises to come, presents to open in a delightful drift of paper and ribbons.

Somewhere in Maine? Hundreds of miles from Bride's Bay?

Or New Brunswick, still almost impenetrably wild in places, pockets of people who spoke only French, or their version of this sublime language. De Lima had once gotten lost in New Brunswick, trying to detour around a torn-up road. He remembered asking for breakfast at an isolated house on the edge of the forest, the little girls in their dusty black convent-school uniforms, the work-worn red-handed mother, the ancient of days (her husband? her father?) deaf, in a fireplace corner.

Would this be a good place for Swain to surface? "*Le pauvre*, we took him in, he didn't speak our language, he didn't seem to know who he was or where he was. So, for farm work, we gave him his daily food and a room in the barn . . ."

For the fourth time de Lima turned over in bed. The linen sheets felt damp and hot; the top one had arranged itself into a mighty crumple under his hip. One forty-five, said the luminous dial of the bedside clock.

Thought was usually refreshing, the brain doing its faultless unseen exercises: plan, scheme, stoop, bend, stretch. Ah. Solution. Usually. But it was a dozen solutions he was struggling with.

What about the brown hair dye? It would take weeks to grow out. Somehow conjure up a white wig identical with Swain's extraordinary hair? Would it look fake? There would be reporters, television cameras, headlines, interviews. There would be a close-up of this amazing story of survival, so close you could count Swain's eyelashes.

Would the whole think look fake? Shout fraud? Not eight

months, not a year after the presumed death, but—

Two weeks after the triumphant retrospective. Two short neat weeks.

What to tell Helena Coe? "The damp air exacerbated Wright's arthritis, now he's thinking of a dry climate, perhaps Arizona—" Break the lease or pay it till next May? Would such openhandedness look odd?

And Alice Smith. But she's another problem, push her out. You can't. She's part of the Swain problem. Tell her she's free to go over Swain's possessions, in—where?—a rented storage room in or near Bride's Bay. First arrange for the storage room. Get the key to her. Then, when she had gotten her scrabbling little person to Bride's Bay and into the storage room, deal with her . . .

The next few days, though, were to be devoted to dealing with Swain. When would there be time, before Thursday, to handle the Alice Smith matter?

Indiscretions from all sides threatening. A slip here, a thoughtless stumble there. Maggie with her telephone call to the dead artist, Alice with every word of it down. From here to forever, the chance of disaster around every corner.

Disaster for Adrian de Lima. Disgrace and ruin for that celebrated and prosperous arbiter of taste, setter of styles, leader in his field, internationally known Adrian Taliaferro de Lima.

Two-seventeen on the clock, and he was nowhere. Not even in his own bed, not feeling the texture of the sheets or the soft lift of the pillow. But in a—was it a sort of daze, or a half-sleeping vision? He seemed to be looking down the possible corridors of his life. This one dim and fogged, rain splashing against dirty windows (were they barred?), weary twists and turns of the passageway waiting, stretches where he could miserably run, angles where he could try to hide himself . . .

The other corridor was pierced with graceful arches, sun pouring in, a scent of champagne so fresh and real it nipped the nostrils. Geraniums ablaze, a strut of peacocks. Heat and light. A shining felicity of the soul and spirit.

New Brunswick?

What about the hair dye?

The people who had taken him in would have to be found,

informed, rehearsed, and then paid for their story. Scrap
them.

A cave somewhere where Swain had taken shelter? But wha
would he have done to feed himself? He didn't know how to
use a gun, shoot birds or rabbits. And in any case where would
he have gotten the gun?

If there had been time, all this would have been able to be
resolved, no weak spots or indeed gaping holes in the carefully
woven fabric. If Swain hadn't got himself shot at. If Swain
hadn't taken it into his head that someone was trying to kill
him.

Someone else.

I have a lot to lose, Adrian. So have I, John. You might put
it as: everything.

At twenty after three he got out of bed, turned on a lamp
and went to look at himself in the pier glass. The mirrored im
age was that of a baffled, exhausted man appearing now a
good deal older than he ought to. But the man standing in
front of the glass was another man entirely, regarding his re
flection with wildly amused contempt. One is either manipu
lated, or one manipulates; life is exactly as simple as that.

Ordinarily polite in his language, and especially so when ad
dressing himself, de Lima said to the other man, in the mirror
"You poor contriving, conniving bastard, lying there racking
your brains like a madman—but you knew it all along, didn'
you? *Didn't you?* Ever since Swain called. Ever since Swain
said, I'm afraid our romp has come to an early end. As of
about a minute from now, Adrian, I am John Swain."

Swain thought he must have fallen asleep for twenty
minutes or so; he'd lost a little patch of time. Around the
edges of the closely drawn shades a lightening showed the ap
proach of dawn. There was no time to be lost now. The sooner
he got out of here the better. Putting the flashlight on the
kitchen floor, he made coffee double strength, drank two cups
of it, showered and shaved. He put on John Wright's slightly
worn and undistinguished gray suit, a white shirt, and a dark
blue tie. He polished John Wright's black wing-tip shoes with
paper tissues, brushed John Wright's brown hair, and went to
the telephone.

There was no chance, was there, that wires might have been fiddled with and the thing could blow up in his face? His body seemed to him merely a collection of nerves. His skin felt crawling and itchy and he could feel a pulse beating in his temple. Ada Garble, he had noticed before, was an early riser. And if she hadn't been she would be, this morning.

It was shortly after five o'clock. She answered in a voice that suggested recent sleep and uncombed hair.

"Sorry to bother you at this hour, but something's come up. My brother-in-law's been in a car accident and my wife's sister is in a panic. She called me just now. I must go and see what's to be done. Could you possibly drive me to the bus station in Lakewood, the earlier bus the better?"

He had first considered asking her to drive him all the way to New York but he couldn't face the probing, the opportunities for questions, for conversation, for further remembrances of the art instructor at St. Elizabeth's. His brother-in-law, he had decided, lived in Norwalk, Connecticut; if asked by her he would say he'd take a train from Grand Central.

To erase the open broadcasting of flight to anyone passing by, or lingering, he left lights on in the kitchen and the bedroom. Take no luggage. Tell Ada that he expected to be back tomorrow or the next day. Keep her by his side in the bus station until departure time, until he could scramble into his seat and hide behind a newspaper.

In twelve minutes her car was at the foot of the cement walk. He ran, heart pounding, down the walk. "Not that much of a hurry, John," she said. "We've got time and to spare. You poor thing you look as though you hadn't slept a wink. When did you get the call?"

"Around four."

"Probably skipped your breakfast." She touched a metal lunchbox on the seat between them. "I brought you a stickybun, not heated I'm afraid, and some coffee. Careful, don't spill it."

Good woman, kind woman—used woman; he must, when his personal smoke cleared, send her something in the way of thanks.

It was a half hour's drive, over the causeway to the mainland and through commuters' towns already busy with cars heading for New York, for the bus station, for the naval installation at Lakehurst.

"Stay with me for a bit, Ada? I'm not good at buses and I don't quite know—"

"Poor love. I'll park here, and then we'll go straight to the ticket window." Lots of people, thank God, seething around in a patternless way. The New York-bound bus wasn't loading yet. Swain's darting eyes searched faces from behind his dark glasses. It was reassuring, a little, to think he looked as uninteresting as the rest of them.

"There, they're getting on now," Ada said. He bought a newspaper from a stand a few yards away, walked to the foot of the bus steps, hesitated, then kissed her cheek. She blushed and he saw tears in her eyes. "I hope everything will turn out all right. Remember to eat a decent meal at noon no matter what."

Swain chose a seat by the window near the rear of the bus, which filled rapidly. The seat beside him was taken by a large, formidable black man. Good.

There was a slight tremor through the bus as the driver started his engine. For a second Swain thought the shaking originated in his own nerves.

Lever pulled, front door scissored closed. The second section of the six o'clock bus now began loading.

Matt went by the first bus, which was already moving slowly. He looked anxiously upward, wondering if the second bus was as jammed full as this one.

He saw, a few inches from a window near the rear, John Swain's head, turned away from the glass. John Swain's nose, John Swain's jaw, and then, in a gesture unfolding a newspaper, John Swain's long thin hand.

Impelled on a selected course, without any thought at all, Matt went up the steps of the second bus. Pulling his hat more firmly down on his head, he too took a seat near the rear. The bus in front pulled away, its exhaust sending a stinging reek through its waiting twin.

Matt blinked several times, then got up and made his way, high-arming his duffle bag, down the narrow aisle, oblivious to the glares of entering passengers bearing bulky packages and suitcases.

There was no point in staying on the bus now. There was no
point in heading back to New York, to his job, to Maggie.

There was no earthly point in going anywhere.

"Johanna?"

No answer was possible except a stunned and simple,
"Yes."

She had been up since six, too happy and excited to sleep.
Music on softly, a lazy bath. What did you wear for a morning
visit from Sam Hines? Did you dress, right away, sensibly, for
a stint of gardening in Quogue? Or? She put on a ridiculously
expensive Yves Saint Laurent she had bought with last year's
Christmas bonus. Harem trousers tied at the ankles, a loose
fisherman's-smock blouse, the whole business flowered all
over in tulips and poppies.

When the telephone rang at a little after seven-thirty, she
made a dive for it.

"Johanna?"

After her answering monosyllable, there was a pause of a
second or two. Background noises, as if he were talking from
a large busy echoing place.

He didn't formally identify himself; he knew from her
voice, just that one word, that it was unnecessary.

"I've painted myself, one way or another, into a corner. A
tight one. I need what there are no other words for but a hiding place. A matter of a couple of days. Can I come to you?"

"Yes, of course. Where are you now?" Even through
astonishment that nearly robbed her of breath, an odd
thought knifed: *the last place anyone would think of looking
for me is my own daughter's apartment.*

"Some god-awful bus-dumping place." Swain had never
before been in New York's Port Authority Bus Terminal and
considered it, even without the fear still hurrying every step he
took, a species of hell. "By the way, you're alone? You don't
share an apartment?"

"No. I mean yes, I'm alone."

"Sorry to sound the way I'm going to, but nobody, absolutely nobody but you can know about this, Johanna."

"I . . . yes. Apartment 4G. You have the address?"

"You wrote it down for me at Bride's Bay. There's a cab

stand near me, I won't be more than ten minutes or so."

Twenty-two minutes of eight. She fought a rising panic that right now had nothing to do with her father's impending arrival, or the possible danger he might be in. She dialed Sam's number. After five rings, his telephone service came on. "No message," Johanna said. He had left his apartment. He was on his way here. They were both on their way here.

What if they arrived together?

Please, Sam darling, please, please, get here first, so I can explain.

But I can't explain.

Seven minutes to eight. One ring at the bell. The eyehole in the door showed her what for a moment was a stranger. Feeling an interior trembling, not of fear but of almost unbearable tension, she opened the door.

He came in and closed it behind him. "This is good of you, Johanna," he said, his voice low. "Entirely on trust, as you might say. But that's a two-way street. Oh, and don't pay any attention to the stage makeup." He took off his dark glasses and the tired hazel eyes blazed at her.

"One thing," she said, feeling as though her voice was beating with her racing heart, "There's someone coming, any minute, I couldn't reach him by phone to head him off and this is only as you see—" She flung out an arm to indicate the limits of her one-room apartment. Where the L turned its corner, there was concealment, granted that no one came in at the door.

He walked past her and looked quickly left and right. "But you'll send whoever it is away?"

"Yes. But I think, for now, in here." The door to the dressing area was as always open; it gave the hallway, passing a bank of louvered closets on the left, a liberating sense of at least a little extra space.

Swain went in and silently closed the door behind him.

What, Johanna thought, standing outside it, what if I simply don't answer the next ring, or knock, or however Sam announces himself? Just let the sound repeat, and repeat, inside an empty apartment. Sorry, Sam, no one here, no one at all.

One minute after eight. The doorbell, an aural impact like a shot. I can't. I won't, thought Johanna, hand on the door-knob turning it.

Sam, fresh and dark and raincoated and seeming to have still a whiff of the morning wind about him.

"I'm terribly sorry," Johanna said. "Something's come up and I can't—I mean I have to cancel the whole day and right here at the door, Sam." Her father would, of course, be hearing every word. She could not add, I'll explain it all later, please do trust me.

He looked hard at her. He saw a good deal more than she intended him to see. Some kind of radiance which her emergency had not yet dispelled, making her surrounding air seem to simmer. The pretty, femininely welcoming garments, the flowers of her, the scent. The stricken eyes, stricken he was fairly sure for him.

Right here at the door, Sam. There was, he gathered, someone else in the apartment. A scrambling of schedules, a mis-meeting of lovers wanting Johanna in the morning?

It didn't seem her style.

He couldn't summon up a graceful acceptance of this maddening, this inexplicable dismissal. He thumped the paper bag he was holding onto the floor just outside the door. "The champagne's chilled if you have any immediate use for it," he said, and turned and walked away.

FOURTEEN

"That was Sam Hines, wasn't it," Swain said. "I didn't know you knew him."

Was. Knew. Two apt past-tense syllables.

"Yes."

"Sorry to have gotten in the way of your plans. You don't, you know, have to stay here. I just wanted a roof and walls for let's say forty-eight hours." He went a deep red. Embarrassment, she surprisedly identified it, using the part of her mind that hadn't gone down the corridor to the elevators with Sam Hines. "I want to offer you a few words but I could get them out more easily over brandy, if you have such a thing."

"Yes . . . just a moment . . ." She found she had unknowingly picked up the bottle of champagne. She put it into the refrigerator and poured brandy.

"Do sit down," she said, trying not to sound formal. "I haven't much to go on but you look tired to me."

Swain took a grateful sip of his brandy and went to the slipper chair. Leaning forward, he said, "This is not an apology, or even an explanation, but merely a point of view. Oil companies cap wells against the day prices go up, don't they. American free enterprise and so on. For a short time I capped my own well. It would have stayed that way much longer but—" He decided in mid-sentence to change course. Don't involve her, even verbally, in the reason for his flight. Unfair

156

and, yes, unnecessary. "But someone in New Jersey, in the little town where I was holed up—under another name, of course—thought she recognized me. Did, as a matter of fact, recognize me, although she had yet to cross the final *t*. I had to cut and run."

"Will you find another little hole? Another place?"

"No. Later on this week I will emerge whole and intact from brief amnesia. I'm, by the way, still trusting you. Implicitly. And the less you know about it the better." He got up and went into the kitchen and came back with brandy for her. "I haven't much to go on but you look in a state of shock, Johanna. Drink it down."

She didn't say that the appearance of shock had little or nothing to do with him.

Right here at the door, Sam. The second time I threw you out.

Threw you away.

Grasp the immediate present with both hands. That's the thing to do.

"I must"—alien, bewildering idea—"dress and go to work. First, if there's anything you want I'll telephone for it and wait until it's delivered. There's food, though, and scotch and gin along with the brandy, and cigarettes if you want them. Oh, and a bottle of champagne. Here's the *Times*. The television set has a radio attachment. Books, if you . . ." She gestured at generously filled shelves.

"You're remarkably hospitable to a form of felon," Swain said. "Are you usually much telephoned during the day? I suppose not, if you work."

"No. Except the usual junk calls. If for any reason I have to get in touch with you I'll ring twice, hang up, and then after one minute ring again."

She went into the little dressing room and changed into her black jersey suit. A day for dark glasses; her eyes looked odd, as though there were tears behind them, waiting.

She said, "If anyone rings at the door—parcels or things —they'll leave whatever it is with the superintendent if no one comes. It might be a good idea if you got some sleep."

"I'll try. Inadequate words, but—thank you, Johanna."

* * *

Maggie's sleep was uneven and shallow. She woke often, worrying about Swain. De Lima's reassurances, when she had telephoned him after Swain's call, hadn't stuck.

("My dear Maggie, with houses to either side of him what possible harm could come to him, if, as he plans, he stays put? This hardly being a Mafia matter, we will not look to having his screened porch blown up.")

At five, she said to herself, this is ridiculous, and got up. She knew Swain's secret timidities. He might really have been shot at by some local psychotic, or he might have mistaken the sound; but, alone, he would be riddled with fears and fancies. What he needed was company, another voice, music playing, a shared drink, the world turned cheerfully back to normal.

Not wanting to risk the walk by herself at this dim and empty hour, she hailed a cab and asked the driver to take her to the nearest car rental service. In the green Plymouth she made good time; the heavy traffic was coming into the city, not going out.

She got to Seashell Park shortly after seven o'clock. She knocked a number of times at the front door, then went around and repeated the process at the back. The house felt, even from the outside, empty.

Perhaps he had gone for an early walk. She sat down on the back steps and saw, in the house next door, a window going up. A woman put her head out. "If you're looking for Mr. Wright," she called, "he's gone off to Norwalk, Connecticut." With the relish of one imparting bad news, she went on, "Car accident. His brother-in-law. I drove him to the six o'clock bus to New York. He said he'd take the train from there."

"Oh," Maggie said. "Thank you very much."

Was this de Lima at work already? She drove to a public telephone booth she had passed a few blocks back and called him. His horrified astonishment answered her question.

"*Gone?* To, where, *Norwalk?* Good God."

"One can only assume he was frightened out of his wits after last night and just ran off. And I tend to doubt Norwalk." She gave him the accident report of the next-door neighbor.

Sounding unlike himself, out of breath, his rich voice going high and sharp, de Lima said, "But he assured me that he'd sit tight there for a few days while I made the necessary arrangements—Good God."

"He probably got second thoughts as one does in the ghastly small hours. As *I* did, which is what brought me down here at this hour."

"Well." Word blurred on a sucked-in gasp of air. "He'll probably come running straight to you. You'd better get back as fast as possible. We can't have him sitting all day in full display in the lobby of the Barclay."

"I'm leaving this minute."

De Lima went and took a tranquilizer and then sat down to his breakfast in the blue parlor. Must look, act, and eat, in front of Mrs. Mount, as if this was a perfectly normal de Lima day. Two nicely poached eggs on toast, he ought to be able to get those down.

(Where would Swain go? He hadn't friends all over the map to flee to. If he didn't dash to Maggie, he'd know soon. The six o'clock bus: he'd be in New York now, at close to seven-thirty.)

"Yes, Mrs. Mount, another cup of coffee." He always finished breakfast with fresh fruit. Could he face the chilled honeydew? His appetite was invariably excellent; it must be excellent this morning.

(If he didn't go to Maggie, then where? He'd obviously not had time before his bus to go to the bank, and in any case the money available there was limited. He wouldn't have enough cash in hand to stay at a hotel for more than a day or so.)

A little saucer was placed before him with his vitamin tablets, the B-complex and the C.

(I suppose there's one chance in ten he might come straight to me. No, too risky. From a professional, not a physical, point of view. He would never, no matter how panicked, be fool enough to head for Bride's Bay. His altered looks wouldn't shield him there and anyway his house was probably rented, occupied.)

De Lima thoughtfully touched his mouth corners with his white damask napkin. His firm conclusion was that Swain was and would be unquestionably somewhere in New York, a good city to get lost in, a logical place in which to make a clean-cut escape from some pistol-bearing madman in Seashell Park, New Jersey.

Problem (if he didn't go to Maggie or arrive here at the gallery): to flush him from whatever cover he had chosen to take shelter in.

Johanna's office at around eleven o'clock had its usual Monday-morning gathering of colleagues, drinking coffee, ruminating upon their various weekends, leisurely collecting themselves for the plunge into the work week.

"Dark glasses?" inquired Peter Parnell. "What naughtiness have you been into, Joey?"

She had been on and off trying to fasten her attention to notes on her next assignment, which ought to be interesting but at the moment sounded only wearisome. The relatively new pattern of dental technicians going into business for themselves, cleaning up on cleaning teeth in their own offices. Enraged dentists, threatened with the loss of considerable easy money, were busily instituting suits. The technicians would no doubt be photogenic; they were always pretty girls.

Appearing in the open doorway of her office, Sam Hines said, "I'm sorry I'm late, Johanna, For the Long Island thing. Are you ready!

She was completely undone, and in no condition for introductions and sociabilities. "Yes, I'm ready." She picked up her handbag and the yellow wool pea jacket slung over her chair back. "Sorry, all. Must run."

"The car's down in the UBC bowels," Sam said as they walked along the scarlet-carpeted corridor. "I suppose an elevator will take us to the lower depths? I'll explain all this when"—as they passed a short red-haired man wearing a football jersey and a monocle—"we get away from your executives."

In the car, heading east, he told her about his morning. He had been in such a rage that he forgot he had brought the car down and left it in the parking garage around the corner from her apartment. "I started to walk, or rather, stamp all the way home and then at Forty-third Street I remembered and went back and got it. I was still chewing nails and spitting them out in all directions when I got home."

He had punished the piano for a while, at full pedal; and then he had stopped to think.

All he needed, he saw, was just one leap, one pounce, of intuition, or ESP, or whatever took over when you were that close to someone else.

It did leap. "I knew it had to be Swain, and no one but Swain, in there with you. I telephoned and thought no matter what, you would answer. You would have had time to think up an explanation. But you didn't answer. Nobody did. It was just on the offset off-chance that I headed for UBC. I thought if there were any cloak-and-dagger goings-on you might think it wise to appear to be following your normal schedule. And there you were"—he laughed a little to himself—"*Joey.*"

Taking a quick glance at her readable face, he said, "In case my guess about your guest worries you, you might remember that in this, as well as in any other matter, I am entirely on your side."

The impossibility of denial was an enormous relief. "There's nothing wrong with him and it's only for a few days. He thought someone was on the point of recognizing him in the town where he was living."

"Cramped quarters for two people," Sam said thoughtfully, swinging onto the Triborough Bridge. "Unless they're lovers. Perhaps you'd better stay at my place until he takes himself off. But we'll leave those arrangements until later. Right now, Quogue."

She was glad that he didn't scold, set himself up in judgment on her father's adventures in fraud, warn her of any possible dangers of collusion, concealment. This, he was silently saying to her, is your own business, Johanna.

But right now, right here, joy at the moment and better to come, is our business.

FIFTEEN

"You do realize, Maggie, that this is rather frightful," de Lima said, when by two o'clock Swain hadn't been heard of or from.

With a vague suspicion that she might be concealing Swain in her hotel quarters, he had dropped in on her in her room. He was outwardly calm. Maggie was openly restless, roving the room.

"No, darling," she had said ten minutes earlier, when he made to open a door, "that's my closet, the bathroom's to your right."

"One hopes," de Lima said, now getting up from his chair and reaching for his walnut stick, "that this possibly imaginary assailant hasn't caught up with him."

"I don't think he was imaginary." Maggie ran her fingers through the white swipe in her hair. "And please, Adrian, don't keep calling me because every time you do I think, ah, now, *there* he is. Naturally I'll let you know right away."

De Lima went back to his gallery and locked himself into his office. Go ahead, go through the motions, anyway; action made one feel almost sane. He called his guard Ruggles at the warehouse in SoHo and told him to remove himself and the Dobermans at four o'clock. He was, he said, going to give a little preview-reception there. "I won't need you and your monsters until tomorrow morning. I'll tell Hancock he'll be wanted at eleven o'clock to take over." Hancock was the guard who spelled Ruggles on weekends.

He went back to brain-racking. Would Swain for any wild reason go to Matt Cummings? At least Matt was someone he knew, living in New York. Where? There wasn't any Cummings, Matthew, in the telephone directory.

Could devious Maggie have fixed up something with her nephew, Sam Hines? De Lima had been to a party some time ago at Hines's apartment; big warren of a place, an inherited cooperative, soundproofed because of the pianos. A marvelous hiding place, it would be.

Sam Hines. Sam Hines. Yesterday, in front of an apartment door, 4G, in Murray Hill. That girl opening the door, that girl with her Swain eyes, who had turned out not to be Alice Smith, but authentic and attractive Johanna Landis.

Swain saying, on a windy hillside in Bride's Bay, "I haven't seen her since she was three so I can't evaluate her character." And, when pressed by de Lima, "your own flesh and blood," the harsh "Get off it, will you."

He looked up her number and dialed it. There was no answer.

Keep trying it on and off. Along with anything else he could think of.

Johanna called her apartment at four-thirty, using her two-ring, hang up, and dial again signal. She wanted to know if everything was all right and he said, yes, it was, that he'd been enjoying himself reading her Joyce Cary, *The Horse's Mouth*. She politely outlined her evening schedule. "I'm going out to dinner, I think. I should be back no later than say eleven. There are lamb chops in the freezer compartment, you might take them out right away. You don't mind being alone?"

"Not at all. As a matter of fact, I've been thinking how awkward this is for you, having a total stranger spending the night asleep in your chair in the corner. I thought about suggesting that you go to a hotel for tonight. Nervy of me, but possibly preferable from your point of view."

"No." Too rejecting a gesture, she thought. "We'll manage one way or another. I have a sleeping bag from my younger days in the storage room downstairs. And"—a catch of laughter; how light, floating, her voice sounded, no resemblance to this morning's voice—"we are related, you know."

De Lima, calling during this conversation, heard the busy signal on the line.

He began dialing the number—again nonanswering—every five minutes.

After the seventh call, Swain was tempted, childishly, to cover his ears and shout, Go away and leave me alone!

But the maddening persistence of the phone suggested urgency, emergency, maybe something of vital importance to Johanna. Who, after all, was doing him a colossal favor and doing it in the most graceful and natural way.

Maybe it wouldn't ring again.

It did. He answered it with a breath-squeezed. "Hello."

"Thank heaven, my dear fellow," said de Lima. "Are you prepared to listen, and listen carefully? Our schedule has been moved up, you'll be pleased to hear. First get a piece of paper and a pencil . . . Now then. I'll pass along refinements to you later but what happened to you is as follows. Of course you don't know what went on in the interim, but you found yourself working on a fishing boat out of Hyannis on Cape Cod. You have no idea how long this period lasted. You were let go in Boston and not being in ample funds drifted to a down-at-heels boardinghouse near the docks. I've got a room for you there, waiting. This coming Thursday, you are idling about on a wharf and chance upon an artist sitting at an easel doing a pastel of Boston Harbor. I've commissioned our man and told him the view is wanted by a Boston bank. Light breaks, memory returns. Do something dramatic, like bursting into tears, or perhaps shouting your own name like a madman. Our artist will no doubt get the point and proceed on his own from there. Are you following me so far?"

"Yes. How do I get to Boston?"

"Take a taxi to the SoHo warehouse in plenty of time to be there by six o'clock. The door will be unlocked. Go inside, as you may have a short wait. My trucker will arrive in front of the warehouse soon after six. As far as he's concerned, you're not on board at all. You won't ride in the cab but in back. He will park his truck in front and go in search of a little liquid refreshment before his Boston run. You will slip out the door and into the truck. There's clothing to change into, inside, including a pair of suitably stinking boots covered with fish scales. Money in the jacket pocket, and the address of your boardinghouse, and an alternate date for our artist's pastel sketch if it rains on Thursday, and the location of the wharf he'll be sketching on. When you arrive in Boston, the truck will home in in front of another bar. At this point, you remove yourself from it. You will find your boardinghouse, Mrs. McCreavy's, right around the corner from the bar, on Cheval Street. You aren't, by the way, John Wright anymore for obvious reasons. You are John Winch—you got your name from this fixture on your fishing boat.''

Swain gave a short laugh. "I am dazzled, Adrian, by your flights of villainy. Yes, what else?''

"There are no windows on the main floor of the warehouse and you want to lose no time in getting out to the truck when it arrives. You'll see a flight of stairs which leads to an office, which does have a window. If you find yourself thirsty while waiting, there's a bottle of scotch in the desk drawer. Oh, about your discarded clothing, put it into the rather unsightly suitcase in the truck. Even at a Mrs. McCreavy's it's better to arrive with luggage of a kind. I'm afraid your room there doesn't run to a telephone. Call me from a public booth after you get settled. If you've thought of any questions or complications, we can cover them then. By the way, I assume that at the moment you're alone?''

"Yes, and will be when I leave here.''

"I don't have to tell you not to leave an explicit note?''

"Of course not.''

"Then goodbye and good luck. Although I must say I've left very little or nothing to luck.''

Swain left the apartment at five-thirty, with office-emptying traffic in mind. He left a scribble for Johanna: "I painted myself out of my corner sooner than I expected. Many thanks, Johanna.''

The warehouse fronted on Gillian's Alley, a short narrow street that ran just two blocks. "I'll drop you at the corner, bud, unless you want to spend money going three or four blocks around so we can enter in the right direction,'' the driver said.

The alley was quiet now, at ten minutes of six, and smelled of sour garbage cans. Swain spotted the bar at the far end of the block where his driver would down his beer. Or whiskey. Or both.

He went to the tall wide battered door of Number 21, opened it, and found himself in an immense space under a ceiling towering perhaps thirty feet high. One bare, low-watt light bulb on, in a far corner, near great stacked shipping cartons. He had never visited the warehouse before but knew from de Lima that his thirty canvases, which were to be discovered soon in the barn at Bride's Bay, were in an upper loft reached by a metal-faced freight elevator.

Dust in the air faintly tickled his nostrils. The silence was profound. An old building, brick, solid and stout even if outwardly grimy and Dickensian in appearance. The staircase ran straight up the left-hand wall, almost losing itself in the shadows at the top, where there was the suggestion of an office door, and a long balcony or catwalk arrangement running to its right along the far wall.

His nerve ends began to send him messages. All in his mind, of course. Apart from the peace of Johanna's apartment, the last twenty-two hours had been nightmarish.

He started up the long, steep flight of stairs. Outside the office door, hand reaching for the knob, something made him pause. With the light so dim that the eyes had little to occupy them, and the silence so deep the ears could tell the brain nothing, another sense sharpened and went to work. The sense of smell.

He smelled de Lima.

His own cologne, custom-blended for him in Madrid. A sharp and personal blend of, de Lima had once informed him, geranium and lavender with just a soupçon of tobacco leaf and peppermint.

It spoke his name in the air, at the top of the stairway.

But, good Christ, so what? De Lima probably used the office occasionally. And very probably had been here earlier today, making his arrangements.

Why, though, was the scent so stingingly, so immediately fresh?

To his right were three large trash cans of galvanized metal, standing in front of the freight elevator, which had, he saw, doors opening on the balcony.

Okay, so you're a dithering idiot, round the bend, Swain said to himself, and as silently as he could removed the lid from one of the cans.

I suppose the next thing I'll do is speed up the script, lose the last shred of sanity, and start shouting to the empty warehouse, I'm John Swain! I'm John Swain!

If there was someone in the office, would he wait behind the door when it opened? Ready to attack from the back?

There was of course no one in the office but proceed anyway. He opened the door and took three paces forward. On the third pace—impelled by the instincts which had warned him, armed him—he swung his body, the trash can lid held like a shield. But not quite soon enough.

De Lima's swiftly flashing knife got him in one shoulder and sent him for a few near-fatal seconds staggering off balance. De Lima was blocking the open doorway, knife ready, face expressionless. Grasping the lid with both hands, his face, eyes, and chest covered, Swain flung himself forward. And then, extending both his arms, gave with the lid a shove with all the power of his body and his terror behind it.

For a fraction of time, he was a little bewildered: de Lima wasn't there. Then the thwack of a body hitting somewhere on the stairs below the narrow landing, and the sickening thud, bang, screams of a man going crashing down the steel stairs, and going very fast, to the cement floor below.

Swain stood for a moment fighting a faint. Or was his heart going to attack him and take over where de Lima had left off?

Then he gathered himself and ran down the stairs and made himself look at the sprawl at the bottom, head cocked ominously sideways, eyes closed, blood pouring from a great gash on the forehead. He bent and put a trembling palm close to the open mouth, and wasn't sure whether or not he felt a faint breathing.

He ran back up the stairs. Telephone. Yes, there on the desk. He asked the operator for the police emergency number, dialed 911, and said, "There's a man in a warehouse at 21 Gillian's Alley who has had a bad fall and may be dying," and hung up. Glancing at his hand, he saw a trickle of blood on the back of it: the shoulder wound at work. There was an old raincoat hanging on a hook near the desk. He snatched it and pulled it on and ran down the stairs again. On the next step to the bottom, he saw the knife, picked it up in a kind of reflex action, and pocketed it. There must be a back way out but too risky searching for it. A police car might be a few blocks away right now, getting radioed instructions ". . . and may be dying."

Out the front door, then, and walk, don't run. He reached the bar on the corner, where his driver would soon turn up for his beer or whiskey.

What driver? What truck? What boardinghouse near the docks?

All imaginary, of course. "I am dazzled, Adrian," he had said, "by your flights of villainy."

But would de Lima want the knifed body of even an unimportant man from New Jersey found in his own warehouse? No. Swain cast his mind back to the great packing cartons on the main floor. Get your man into a carton, at leisure, after he was dead, make a workmanlike job of it with a staple gun. Then, drag your carton out the back way into the night, and leave it somewhere near but not connectingly so. A package weighing 160 pounds would be rather burdensome.

He couldn't remember having, in the bar, ordered whiskey but here it was in his hand. He was sitting in a small booth for two at the rear. He kept his bloodied left hand in his pocket while with his right hand he lifted the glass and emptied it. He signaled the bartender for another and then went to the wall phone. Fortunately for privacy, the jukebox up near the front was savagely functioning. ". . . *every time you touch me I could cry . . .*"

Maggie answered right away. He told her fast and with a feeling of disbelief what had happened; as though it had happened to another man.

Her response was swift, and pure Maggie. "Go to—where's the nearest clinic to you? No, make it farther away. Make it St. Vincent's on West Eleventh Street. Get your shoulder bandaged. Say you had a fight with your wife. Is it, do you think, deep—dangerous?"

"No. I can hardly feel it." He put a hand to his shoulder, under his raincoat. "Not even much blood."

"Good. Then it won't turn into a police matter for them at the clinic. After you leave there, take a taxi to Kennedy, if you have enough money on you."

"Yes, I have."

"I'll pack and leave here and join you there. Wait in the Pan Am lounge bar. I'll get tickets to someplace. As a matter of fact, Mary Powell offered me her summer cabin in Flagstaff, in Arizona, to recover from my great loss and grief. Yes, Flagstaff. I'll have the tickets made out to Mr. and Mrs. John Wright. See you soon, darling."

"But I had an appointment with him on Thursday!" was Alice Smith's first outcry when she came upon the report of de Lima's death on page 5 of the Tuesday evening Trenton *Free Press*.

"If people who have anything to do with Swain go around getting their necks broken for them, I'd back off if I were you," Stan said.

"Mmmm . . . it says here that the autopsy showed no trace of alcohol or any other drug . . . police conclude that the noted gallery proprietor and art dealer suffered a dizzy spell at the top of the flight of stairs and . . . Wait a minute. Listen to this. 'In a routine search of the building, police came upon a number of paintings stored in a loft above the main floor of the warehouse. All are signed by the well-known American artist John Swain, who under a month ago was presumed to have lost his life in a sailing accident in a storm off the coast of Maine. One New York expert estimated the market value of this store at well into the millions.' "

She got a pair of scissors and clipped out the half column. "Five years from now you'll be reading about *me*, in court, getting my share," she said. She decided to keep to herself— now that it was no longer of use in prying advance money out of de Lima—the overheard telephone call. It wouldn't do to raise any questions of fraud, of whether or not Swain was really dead.

It might affect the market value of his paintings.

In the same issue of the *Free Press* was a small item, on page 18. "BODY OF MAN FOUND ON BEACH. A man identified as Matthew Cummings, of New York City, was discovered by joggers this morning on a lonely stretch of beach north of Seashell Park. His gun was still in his hand. Police describe it as a clear case of suicide."

Dear Johanna,

I thought it was unfair to have you spending your life, or at least a little of it, wondering if your father might be a murderer. In writing this, I am of course putting my own life in a way into your hands but it feels for some strange reason secure there—seeing we know superficially so little about each other.

I was defending myself against a deliberate attempt at murder, on de Lima's part, and in the course of this defense he managed to lose his own life and not mine.

As far as the future goes, John Swain will remain drowned, so therefore I do pay for my sins (among which I do not include de Lima's tumble). But his untimely end made it all too risky, from the point of view of any possible deep investigation, to continue with our little as he called it—romp.

I have always wanted to try my hand at sculpture. Sometime, who knows? you may be hearing of a new if elderly talent in this line, man by the name of John Winch. I am now in possession of one hundred pounds of clay. And, sometime, John Winch might invite Johanna Landis, or whatever her last name is then, to an opening (*not* a retrospective) in the Southwest. He will have his white hair back but his parrot's beak—and I'll miss it—will be classically straight. As, come to think of it, yours is. With love, J (S) W

Mary McMullen, who comes from a family of mystery writers, was awarded the Mystery Writers of America's Best First Mystery Award for her book *Strangle Hold*. Her other books include *The Other Shoe, Something of the Night, My Cousin Death, But Nellie Was So Nice,* and *Welcome to the Grave.* She and her husband live in Albuquerque, New Mexico.

★★★★★★★★★★★★★★★★★
WINNER OF THE MYSTERY
WRITERS OF AMERICA AWARD
MARY McMULLEN
★★★★★★★★★★★★★★★★★

"Entertaining...Charm and suspense in
equal measure." — Kirkus Reviews

"Unusual." — Chicago Tribune

"Jolting suspense." — Publishers Weekly

*Don't miss these
extraordinary mysteries by
America's preeminent Whodunit author.*

___06671-1	THE GIFT HORSE	$2.95
___08752-1	SOMETHING OF THE NIGHT	$2.95
___08834-X	A GRAVE WITHOUT FLOWERS	$2.95
___08905-2	UNTIL DEATH DO US PART	$2.95
___08956-7	THE OTHER SHOE	$2.95
___09051-4	BETTER OFF DEAD	$2.95

Available at your local bookstore or return this form to:

 JOVE
THE BERKLEY PUBLISHING GROUP, Dept. B
390 Murray Hill Parkway, East Rutherford, NJ 07073

Please send me the titles checked above. I enclose _____. Include $1.00 for postage
and handling if one book is ordered; add 25¢ per book for two or more not to exceed
$1.75. CA, NJ, NY and PA residents please add sales tax. Prices subject to change
without notice and may be higher in Canada. Do not send cash.

NAME_____

ADDRESS_____

CITY_____STATE/ZIP_____

(Allow six weeks for delivery.)